Bonded with an

ALIEN
FEMALE

Eduard Schrama

ARCHWAY
PUBLISHING

Archway Publishing books may be ordered through booksellers or by contacting:

Archway Publishing
1663 Liberty Drive
Bloomington, IN 47403
www.archwaypublishing.com
1 (888) 242-5904

ISBN: 978-1-4808-4715-6 (sc)
ISBN: 978-1-4808-4716-3 (e)

Library of Congress Control Number: 2017907583

Print information available on the last page.

Archway Publishing rev. date: 7/5/2017

Contents

Preface

An encounter at a flea market in Holland, the country of my birth, drastically changed my future. I emigrated to America at age twenty four, and at seventy I decided to take my last trip to Holland. I've always found these markets interesting, and as usual spent the afternoon resisting the urge to carry useless items home. As the stalls emptied, an old man remained with his place still fully loaded with items. Strangely, I had the urge to ask why he had not left.

"I have an item that has tremendous value for the right person, and I think you may be the one," he said. He produced an old computer monitor and convinced me to have him demonstrate its powers. The monitor produced shocking images from my past, and he urged me to take it home to America. "Guard it well. It's a valuable instrument," he said. His demonstration made enough of an impression to convince me to promise him I would care for it.

Upon my return home, I forgot the strange episode until the old man knocked on my door, accompanied by a stunning looking female. "We're here to explain the mission you'll be part of," the man said.

In passing, he mentioned that they were from another world. "Don't be shocked. We have observed you since birth," the man said.

Casually, the female mentioned she'd be living with me as my partner in this endeavor. They cloned me, giving me a younger exterior and fused my brain with the female's brain. I became an instant savant.

We traveled to major universities in Europe and visited defense facilities in the Far East. We completed the assignment they had, and I settled with my partner on Long Island, New York, enjoying the fruits of our successful completion of a mind-blowing episode.

The Flea Market

I had left Holland, the country of my birth, many years ago and wanted to return once more to visit my nephew and family. My immediate family and friends had passed or moved, and I had no desire, other than to visit my old neighborhood once more to satisfy my curiosity.

I had emigrated to the US at age twenty four and settled with my wife on Long Island, New York. I was not nostalgic about the surroundings in my old hometown. It had been sixty five years since I'd lived through World War II in our family's home, experiencing trying times. However, standing in front of the old house did not disturb me, which was surprising since my recollections were still vivid.

I bought a newspaper, mostly to check for local news events. Something caught my eye as I scanned the pages—an ad for a flea market, spread across the back page of the paper. I liked a flea market atmosphere. The antique road show on American television, where people obtained treasures for a few dollars, was solidly associated with my searching through junk at these markets. I decided to spend the next day at this place. I had a house full of junk, much of which needed to be thrown out, and had a limit of two suitcases on the flight back to the United States. Why look for more stuff I didn't need? Realistically, I knew that unless I found something small and easy to transport I would be going to the market only to satisfy my curiosity.

······●······

A shabbily dressed old man was alone at one of the stalls, and no customers roamed around his area. It was late in the afternoon, and I couldn't understand why he was not packing up. I decided to ask him.

Surprisingly he spoke to me in English. "So you finally decided to come see me. Let me know if you prefer English or Dutch. Either one will do for me."

How does he know that I live in the United States and usually speak English? Is this guy some sort of mind reader?

"Don't look surprised. We know everything about you," he said upon seeing my startled expression.

Who are we? I wondered.

"I have seen you going all over the place during the day and just waited until the time was ripe for you to visit me. I have something that has great value for the right person, and you have been selected."

I was disturbed by his attitude and confrontational style but also curious about his intentions. Was he in some sort of disguise? And what was the organization he alluded to? *They picked me out to do what? Maybe it's smuggling drugs?*

"Allow me a few minutes to explain," he said. I was becoming convinced that this was another nut pushing his worthless stuff. It was late and cold, and I was tired. I wanted to go home.

He kept insisting that I listen to him, and I figured a few more minutes wouldn't do much harm.

"The item I have is fragile; you'll have to take it to your country."

When he hinted at the United States again, I stopped him. "How do you know I'm just visiting? I'm dressed like the natives and speak fluent Dutch. Only someone with a flair for languages would be able to detect my slight accent."

"Never mind. My job is to convince you to buy this item and thereby prove to us that you're the chosen one. Let's get this over with and then I'll answer your questions, as far as I'm allowed."

This whole process was throwing me off balance. How could this man know that I was just visiting my old country? I looked at him, surprised and puzzled, and he laughed.

"We know everything about you, and you were specifically selected for this endeavor a long time ago."

His attitude was both disturbing and intriguing. What could he have that was so valuable, and how did he know that I was just here for two weeks?

He started rummaging through his cardboard boxes and pulled out an ancient-looking computer monitor. "This, my son, has immense value in the proper hands and can avert many disasters in the future."

This guy is crazy and talks in riddles, I thought. But for some reason, that was not enough to make me walk away. It felt almost as if I was being directed to listen to him. He did not make me nervous, even though by now the market was almost deserted. I felt I had to listen to him.

The Monitor

H e took the old computer monitor out of the cardboard box and placed it carefully on his table. He made no effort to look for the usual CPU, keyboard, mouse, and cables. By now I was convinced that under no circumstances would I buy this worthless piece of junk. My attitude did not seem to bother him. He just cleared the table of the leftover stuff that had not been sold.

I attempted a sarcastic remark, asking him if it had been worthwhile standing in the raw weather without making many sales. "My purpose for being here was not to sell anything," he told me. "I'm here to interest you in buying this monitor for five dollars. That will make my day, and it's sufficient."

"It's not the price that's the issue here. What am I to do with an ancient device that is probably defective? I have no use for it. But if you can explain that, I'll take it off your hands for five bucks."

"Okay. Deal," he replied.

I was standing in the cold weather arguing with someone who had told me his only purpose was to interest me in taking this piece of junk off his hands. I'd retired from a good job in the United States and was financially secure. I wasn't rich, but was always able to leave generous tips in restaurants and donate to worthwhile causes.

Why not give this guy his five dollars and make him happy? I can always throw this thing away.

"Come here and stand next to me," he said, pointing at the monitor, which he'd placed at the center of the empty table. I was reluctant to get close to him. With my cynical nature, I expected him to stink. It surprised me that he exuded no odor at all. Standing next to him, he told me to absorb what he was about to show me and wait to ask questions until later. I was getting nervous about this whole situation and felt a strong urge to leave.

"Don't be nervous. Nothing bad will happen to you. We'll just have to make sure that you're suited for the task that lies ahead."

The ridiculousness of this situation suddenly hit me and I wanted to get away. But I couldn't move. I was in the middle of a nearly empty market place with a nut, listening to his sales spiel, and I had lost my ability to move.

"If you pass this test, everything will be explained. I know you're getting anxious but be assured that no harm will be inflicted. I have been instructed to test you, and you cannot leave until I have completed this procedure."

I was now beginning to question my sanity. *Procedure—what does that mean?*

Before I could answer my own question, he asked me. "Is there any event from your past that you have suppressed in your mind and have not discussed with anyone?"

"Yes. There are plenty of events I would rather not be reminded of."

"Good. Select one from your early years and one from after you were married."

It did not require much of an effort for me to think back to the war period. I had recently completed my autobiography and recalling episodes from my life had been very stressful. When I was seven years old, my family had sent me out to steal yarn from the wheel bearings of train cars that were parked on an industrial terrain. The trips had to be made in the evening during harsh winter weather, with howling winds and blinding snow. I was the only one familiar with the area, since I explored this rail yard frequently during my daily bicycle trips. I had three older brothers who hid in our crawl space under the house, because the Germans arrested males from sixteen years up for deportation to Germany. My mother used the yarn to knit sweaters, which were ideal for bartering for food with local farmers. The trips were made in the dark and were dangerous, requiring all my fortitude. I guessed these were the conditions he was referring to.

The second event in my past I considered extremely difficult to be reminded of was my son's untimely death from cystic fibrosis. That was buried deep in my mind and was a terrible period I would rather not relive.

"Put your hand on the monitor and think about those periods in your life that you would rather not recall," he said.

I was standing in front of the monitor, and I decided to follow his instructions and finish this weird happening. As I touched the glass, I saw myself as a young, skinny kid, struggling through a blinding snowstorm, pulling my sled with two buckets of tools, on my way to the rail yard. After a few seconds, the image showed my brothers returning from their nightly trip to farms with their bicycle side bags fully loaded with vegetables.

I was extremely disturbed by the images and took my hand off the glass. How was it possible that this monitor could dig up these ancient happenings?

"Let's look at the second event in your life," said the old man. "Put your hand back on the front of the monitor."

When I touched the top of the case, a clear image appeared again. I was standing next to my son's hospital bed at the time the nurses had prepared my wife and me for his passing. "He will not make it through the weekend," I heard a nurse say. This image had haunted me for a long time, and I had finally been able to bury it. Now I was reliving it as if it just happened. It was a terrible feeling.

The old man saw my reaction when I looked at the images and said, "You passed."

"Passed what?" I reacted; I was stunned. Reliving these events was extremely disturbing to me, and I just wanted to get away from this guy. I was now free to move, and he was smiling broadly.

"I'm so happy I found you. We didn't expect our search to be successful. I shall now explain what this is all about and why it was so important to find you."

"How did you get your information about me?" I asked. "I have never discussed these episodes with anyone."

"Well, you described your life quite well in the autobiography. What you wrote did reinforce our determination to convince you to assist us."

"Assist you with what? How can an old guy like me help you with anything worthwhile?"

"We know that you're not the most patient person we've encountered, but you have to be ready to receive our explanation about the role you'll play in our future travels. I assume that you have determined yourself that this monitor is not an old, useless device, but instead has extraordinary capabilities."

"Yeah, I just figured that out on my own. Thank you. You just have to do some convincing to make me buy it from you."

"That's fair," he said.

"Only the right person can make the device perform as intended, and the test determined that you're the one. You'll have to take it with you to America and, upon arrival, will be instructed about its full capabilities. I know you're presently doubtful about this process, but everything will be cleared up in the future."

He boxed the rest of his contents, which had been spread out over the table, and was ready to leave.

I was getting agitated and tried to corner him, but he just smiled and told me to be patient.

"It will all be explained in due time. Don't worry. Go home and be ready to be instructed. I have boxed the device, and it will be easy to carry. Don't let it out of your sight."

Before I could ask him another question, he loaded up his cart and left. I stood in the open area, alone with a cardboard box that would, according to the old man, affect my future.

Inexplicably, curiosity was now the main ingredient in my mind. All nervousness was gone.

The Trip Home

When I got to my nephew's home, my family had few questions about my day's events, and I didn't have to explain the strange happening at the market. They probably would have questioned my sanity. I stayed one more day and was on my way to Schiphol, the main international airport in the Netherlands. I hand carried the cardboard box and was immediately shunted aside by customs. They made me open the box and explain what it contained. The newspapers warned that anything even remotely suspicious would be confiscated by the Dutch airport authorities, and I had no idea how to explain my strange carry-on luggage. "I'm interested in old computer equipment and found this at a flea market," I told them.

They made me open the back cover, and to my great surprise, it was practically empty. I had been reluctant to check it at home, out of concern I could damage the inside components. The motherboard had one small card plugged in. Otherwise, it was empty. It was clear to the custom's officer that I was not hiding anything inside, and I was cleared to board with my unusual cargo. Hurdle number one overcome.

Customs in the United States had more questions and also inspected the inside of the monitor case to assure that I was not smuggling illegal products into the country. The US officials had the same expressions on their faces as the Dutch Custom's officers had when they found that I was carrying an ancient piece of junk from Europe to the United States. "Another crazy," was probably their conclusion.

Even though I had seen with my own eyes how this monitor had accessed my mind, I was unsure whether this was all some sort of hallucination. Maybe my seventy-year-old brain was starting to go south.

For a month, I expected to receive a message or some other type of contact, and slowly, the strange affair faded from my mind. Even though the recollection and display of my thoughts had made an impact on me, I decided to forget about the strange occurrence.

One more week went by with no contact, and I was becoming certain that the whole affair had been a farce. That feeling was immediately neutralized when the front doorbell rang. I almost fell over when I opened the door. There was the old man, impeccably dressed and accompanied by a female companion.

Why Me?

"Can we come in?" the man said, already pushing himself halfway through the open doorway.

What could I say? I was taken completely by surprise and, in my most sarcastic tone of voice, said, "Of course. Come right in and be comfortable." The man smiled, and the woman stared at me.

This appearance at my doorstep threw me off balance, which was annoying. During the previous month I'd decided that, on the off chance he would show up, I would insist that he get lost with his monitor and wild ideas. Now, with him standing in front of me in my living room, I found myself unable to give him any argument whatsoever. My resistance had been neutralized, partly because of his female companion.

They looked at me for a long time without saying a word. The female was staring at me with a questioning expression, as if she was wondering what was so special about me. I certainly had no idea why they'd decided on the visit. He finally asked how I had digested the confusing way in which I'd met him, and the importance of the monitor. It seemed that his primary concern was not me but, instead, the empty monitor case that I had added to my junk in the basement.

"I hope you took good care of this very important tool we gave you to safeguard."

"Yes. You don't have to worry. It is safely stored with my other valuables," I assured him.

We were standing in the living room, and I was unsure how to handle the situation. The woman had been observing me, and I began wondering what her role was going to be in this strange setup.

"We owe you an explanation. But not everything can be told, at least not yet," the guy explained. "Let me first tell you that we're not from this planet, which I'm sure you had begun to wonder about. We have visited here and lived among the population for a long time, but ours has mostly been a monitoring function. Until recently, we weren't concerned about the direction in which your population was progressing, but lately, your world's events require us to intervene."

"What do you mean by intervene? Are you going to attack earth?"

"No, nothing that drastic is planned. We operate under a set of cosmic laws that prohibit direct interference with internal affairs in other worlds. But we're allowed to investigate and, if possible, influence the authorities who determine their politics."

"Like the United Nations?" I asked.

"Yes, that could be one organization."

"And what do I have to do with all this? I'm a simple immigrant who settled here. I have no special abilities. It doesn't make sense to me."

"Well, you'll soon realize that we have methods at our disposal that will give you a set of capabilities that allow you to interact with anyone, at any technical or intellectual level."

"You're planning to give me a brain transplant? No thanks."

The man, and the woman both laughed, and she said to me. "I'm going to be living with you and will be your companion in all your endeavors."

"If you don't mind, can you be a little more definitive. What is your definition of companion?"

"I'll be your partner in everything you do in the future. I have known you nearly all your life and have always felt an attachment to you. I want to be close to you at all times," she said.

What she meant was hardly open to interpretation.

The outrageous statements the two of them were making rapidly annoyed me. "How can you have known me all my life? I'm twice as old as you."

"Looks can be deceiving," she said.

"Well, here's my point. You can't barge into my house and assume that I'll buy your insane ideas. I think you should just leave me alone. I'm happy with my existence and don't need female companionship."

They seemed to be undeterred by my outburst. They gave me the kind of smile one gives children who behave unpleasantly. It was disturbing, but it also piqued my curiosity.

What can these two crazies want from me that's important enough for them to show up unannounced and insist that I listen to their proposal?

She looked directly at me and said, "We're not crazy."

Is she a mind reader? I wondered.

I realized that they were determined to make their case, and I was getting curious about their purpose for visiting me. *Why not listen to them? I could use a good laugh.*

"That's a good decision," said the female, displaying a sensual smile.

Now that I had adjusted a little to my strange visitors, I took a good look at her. She was strikingly attractive and elegantly dressed. About thirty years old, I guessed, and about my height, with an exotic appearance. *I wonder what her companionship entails.*

"In due time, you'll find out," she said, standing directly in front of me, nearly touching.

Now I was sure she was reading my mind. I started to feel that I was in for a rough emotional ride with this one.

This was becoming an insane situation. *I'm in the autumn of my life, enjoying a peaceful existence, and these two are ready to screw it up.* "Let me ask you a question. How is it going to look, when a seventy-year-old guy has a young woman living with him? You should be aware that it will raise eyebrows. It is not a situation that's easily accepted."

"We know that, and it will be taken care of."

"Great. Are you now hinting at plastic surgery for me?"

"Don't worry; nothing of the sort."

Initially, when they had shown up, I'd assumed I could refuse whatever they had in mind, but my defenses seemed to be weakening by the minute. I took another look at her. She had unusual eyes—very light and intense—and I had the feeling that she looked right through me. It was unsettling and pleasant at the same time.

The old guy seemed to have been lost in thought for a while and suddenly spoke up. "What I'm going to tell you will be difficult to believe, but I think we owe you this explanation. We're from another dimension and have the ability to travel between yours and ours instantaneously. We're governed under universal laws and have constraints placed on us that are strictly adhered to by our world."

Here it comes— Twilight Zone stuff.

"The political structures and events on your planet have become a great concern to us. Our worlds are connected in ways I'm not allowed to divulge. But I can tell you this: If your world self-destructs, it will be extremely detrimental to our existence, and we won't allow that to happen. That's the reason we've contacted you. We have the technology to affect the advances that have been made with the destructive weaponry your countries have developed. That's where you and Jane come in; you will be the technical team that will delay, and ultimately curtail, weapon development progress."

Jane

S o, my assigned female companion had a name. I would accept her company but had trouble believing the rest of their story. I thought their explanation came straight out of Hollywood. Visitors from another dimension, stopping destructive forces on earth with an empty, ancient computer monitor. Sure, give me another drink.

Jane was standing in front of me. She was very direct and showed not a trace of uneasiness. The way she looked and acted with confidence convinced me that I would have shied away from making a pass at her in my younger days. She was totally out of my league. I did not think that in my wildest dreams I could ever have a chance with this woman. She smiled and stared at me. It made me uncomfortable, and I think she noticed it. "When I'm your companion, you'll develop an attraction toward me. I already feel an attachment to you that I'm convinced will get stronger over time," she said.

This situation was becoming bizarre. My unannounced visitors had jammed a weird situation down my throat, and I had the feeling that I had no choice but go along. "Listen, you burst into my house and give me those outrageous reasons for cooperating with you, and you have not given me proof that you're from another dimension. Why should I believe you? I don't want anyone as my companion, and you shouldn't assume that I'll accept your explanations without proof. I don't like uninvited company in my house, for your information."

"Okay, a small demo will suffice to convince you," said the man.

At that instance, they both disappeared, evaporating in front of my eyes. I stood in the living room, bewildered by their disappearance. A knock on the front door woke me out of my shocked existence.

"Do you believe us now?" the man asked with a big smile as they walked in, like nothing unusual had just happened. "Please, don't be upset with us; we're prepared to explain everything."

Even though I was close to believing their explanations, I did not want to be forced into accepting objectionable conditions. "I'm bothered by your companion's behavior, and this has to be clarified before I agree to assist you," I said to the man. I figured I should hold nothing back. Hopefully, they wouldn't like my attitude and would leave me alone. No reaction from either of them. No matter my objections or my responses to their proposal, nothing seemed to deter either one.

Finally the old man spoke. "Okay, let me explain her role and our interactions with you. My assumed name on earth is Aaron. My actual name is Anryna. Her actual name is Andryna. Her earth name is Jane. We treat interactions between the two sexes differently than you, and Jane has been indoctrinated to understand your way of life. She will comply with all your wishes."

Comply with my wishes? You must be kidding. "You're joking right? In my younger days, I've done and seen it all. I'm over the hill and just want to be left alone in that department."

He continued with his description of Jane. "In our world, she's a leader and a member of the National Science Academy. She's exceptionally gifted."

How am I going to function with a female who can run rings around me intellectually?

My thoughts were apparently picked up by both because they laughed out loud and acted as if my concern was hilarious. I was more confused than ever.

"Let me give you a little background. We have been integrating with the earth population ever since you established organized civilizations.

Both male and female members from our dimension have lived on earth and intermarried. Two of the better-known females from your world were Josephine Bonaparte and Marilyn Monroe. Both these women were what you would consider beautiful, and we've structured Jane's appearance after them."

No wonder she's so incredible looking. I would have a stunning-looking beauty with a sky-high IQ living with me. "You certainly know how to get my attention. Are those two the only people I'm aware of who had well-known positions among us?"

"No, many movie stars and leaders in your major educational institutions are also from our world. We've attempted to introduce our people into your government, especially Congress, but that has failed practically every time."

"I'm not surprised. To survive in congress requires representatives to be able to make deals that aren't necessarily in the best interest of their constituents. Many times they hide the real reasons for approving measures rather than presenting an honest assessment of the situation to their voters."

Now that it had been explained what Jane's role was, I still found it hard to believe their explanation. But I was also concluding that I wouldn't get an answer that would satisfy me. *You might as well accept it, buddy. You're going to have a knockout beauty in your life.*

For now, I decided to concentrate on the mysterious capabilities of the monitor. "Why is an empty, old monitor case, with a single circuit board so important to you?"

"It's by no means empty. We've been living among you for millennia, but we can be invisible and undetectable in any way we want to. We're allowed to influence your progression but cannot physically intervene. This monitor is crammed with technology that is invisible to you, since it is from our dimension. It can only be operated by you if we require physical interactions with your world."

Now it started to make a little more sense. *They could not intervene directly and needed me to do the dirty work.*

"That is not how you should look at it," said Jane. She looked annoyed.

"There is another thing that bothers me. Why did you pick me? There is nothing special about me, and it doesn't make sense."

"On the contrary, it makes a lot of sense to us. We've had our eyes on you, ever since you were born. Certain people among your population have qualities that they themselves are not aware of, but we recognize as special. It has nothing to do with outstanding intelligence or physical makeup. It's a supplement to your five senses that only few possess. You were born with this, but it didn't automatically mature. It grows in inner strength through actions and living a moral existence. We have observed you from a young age and have been impressed by your fortitude during the World War II years and subsequent upheavals in your life. Jane was especially interested in you."

I guessed that they were referring to the war years when I was the only one in the family who could obtain barter materials for food exchanges with farmers. In my later years, I had written an autobiography, and they seemed to be aware of that.

"The fact that you obtained an undergraduate and master's degree at a local university at night, while working a full-time job and having a sick child and semi-invalid wife to take care of—that was especially impressive. And this was all accomplished having a limited English language ability and in less time than full-time day students. Don't ask why we selected you. It should be obvious."

Man, they know everything about me. It was simultaneously pleasing and disturbing.

"We were especially amused when you finally decided to put your life story on paper. You were never impressed by your own accomplishments, but fortunately others disagreed. We had attempted to egg you along, but you had resisted our efforts well. It pleased us that you were able to access the depths of you mind and put your journey into words. That convinced us even more that you have the essential component for our task that lies ahead."

So they have effectively tracked me all my life and prepared me for this insane adventure by manipulating my mind? "What if I refuse to help you," I asked. "Will you turn me into a zombie?"

"We're not worried about that. You will not refuse to help us because of your moral makeup. You understand that it's necessary to intervene in the destructive path that's being followed by some nations in your world. It has been of great concern to you."

It was true. Developments in the world had bothered me, and I hoped that the nuclear powers would come to their senses. But weapon proliferation continued unabated.

"We need you because you've shown to be a smart survivor who can make this effort a success. Jane will explain in detail the logistics of our plan, and she will, within reason, comply with your wishes and answer your questions. I have to depart but am always near. I'll be back at a moment's notice, when required."

He went out the front door, and I was alone with this beauty. I expected to wake up any moment from the outrageous dream, but it didn't happen. She was real and in front of me, smiling. She was so close I could detect her scent. *Could this be the way she smells naturally?* Her smell was familiar, but I could not understand why. Was it some sort of perfume I remembered from my younger days?

"Don't be upset," said Jane. "We copied your wife's natural fragrance to make you feel more comfortable with me."

I had always loved the way my wife smelled, and they knew it. It was one of many things I missed about her after she died.

I was getting exceedingly uncomfortable with the situation and Jane's closeness in the living room. I wanted to be alone to digest the crazy adventure I was in. Before I could do anything, Jane told me to go to bed.

"Humans need their sleep. I don't."

Was that a slip of the tongue, or was she conveying something about her nature? I was so exhausted that nothing bothered me anymore. I went into the bedroom, closed the door, and was out in a minute.

Reality

I had a restless sleep but never woke up throughout the night. I slept for nearly ten hours. After the bathroom break, teeth brushing, and gargle, I found Jane in the living room with one of my cats on her lap. She looked expectantly in my direction, as if she needed some acknowledgement or maybe acceptance of the situation. But I didn't want to broach the subject. To me it was as unreal and wild as it had been the day before.

"Aren't you tired?" I finally asked to break the silence.

"I never get tired and don't need rest or sleep, like you."

"Are you an android or some other machine?"

"No. But even though I have a different makeup in my world, right now, I consist of the same flesh and bone as you. Feel free to touch me if you want."

"No thanks. I'll stay in the 'hands-off' department with you, if you don't mind."

"Well, I do mind. I want you to like me and be comfortable with my presence when I'm close to you."

I sat next to her on the couch, and I sensed her nice, familiar fragrance.

"I know you love the way I smell. I insisted on it, because it would make you feel comfortable with me. We know precisely what your likes and dislikes are, and my function is to please you. Research determined what was needed for me to be to your liking."

"You sound like a machine that was built to my specifications. It makes me uncomfortable. Don't take this personally, but I find all this hard to believe. You must understand. I'm too old to get physical with you."

"We expected your reaction and have a solution for you. When Aaron tried to explain our plans to you, we realized that you weren't ready for that type of discussion. Are you now?"

"No. I'd like to defer that until I have adjusted to this unreal situation you've put me in."

"I have infinite patience and will honor you wishes. I suggest you rest a while, until Aaron returns."

The Explanation

I rested an hour, and then Jane appeared at the side of my bed. "Don't you know what privacy means?" I said. "Yes, but you might as well get used to having me around under all conditions. I don't expect you to have any secrets from me." Wow. I swallowed a few times and went into the living room. "Aaron will arrive soon. He'll give you an outline of our plans and what your part will be. He has already explained that the destructive path of the nations on earth is having ramifications in our dimension, and our leaders have made the decision to disrupt it at all cost. Until now, the intervention by us had been deemed to be sufficient to slow down progress in the development of more advanced weaponry, but direct physical actions are now necessary."

I decided to stop her right there. "If you can't intervene physically, who will do it? You better not assume that I'll do that part of the job."

"Let me finish. You can object when I'm done," she said and continued before I could reply. "We've observed weapon research on earth and know how to affect progress, but you have to access their systems since we're not allowed to. We're going to tour some of the foremost scientific institutions in your world, and you'll be introduced as a professor of high energy physics and mathematics, with incredible credentials in the academic world. You'll be presented initially to academia at universities in England, and it will stir immense interest in the research you're involved with."

"You expect me, with my puny brain, to give presentations at universities? Have you lost it?" She ignored my reaction and continued. "Your present position will be the department head of physical sciences in Leiden, a city in the country of your birth. Background investigations will indicate an impeccable research record and an impressive collection of scientific accomplishments in the important European scientific literature. Aaron will be in charge of making adjustments to the university's records. Much of your research will be presented as classified and having been performed at the highest classification levels. It's not available to anyone. No one will be able to question your background, and they'll be wondering where you've been hiding, with all these impressive endeavors in your past."

Yeah, and I'll be wondering myself how I can ever pull this off.

"I realize that this is an outlandish track we've designed for you, but you have to make an indelible impression when you present your research. I'll explain how you can function effortlessly in these high-powered scientific circles without having any chance of being uncovered as the interface to our world. I promise you this. You will confidently, and expertly, integrate with theoretical physicists at any university." My objections were quite feeble at this point. She was so convincing and sure that it seemed useless to object. I decided to make a last point, probably just for the record. "Look, I took a few physics courses during my undergraduate years in college, but they were not at any level that allows me to grasp the research by some of the top minds in the physics world. Besides, that was some fifty years ago; I don't remember much."

"I can assure you that you'll have all the necessary knowledge at your fingertips, and I'll always be at your side to assist you. You'll be safe at all times. Your brain is capable of functioning at the same level as mine. The only difference is that most humans cannot access their full mental capacities. People who have that ability are called savants, and they can perform extraordinary processing in very specialized fields like mathematics and music. We can unleash the full unused capacity of your brain, and in due time, that will be done with you. You'll be what's commonly referred to as a genius in many areas, especially physics and mathematics."

"Let me tell you something. I don't look forward to having you people poke around in my head. As it is, I'm content with my mental capabilities and don't want them increased, or reduced, by you. As you pointed out, I can walk away from this whole crazy process at any time, so don't force anything on me."

"I come from a nonviolent, advanced civilization, and whatever happens to you will be because you decided on your own that you're ready to assist us in removing imminent threats to your and our world. The decision is totally up to you." I became inclined to trust her a little more, even though the fantastic prospects she had discussed were something straight out of *The Twilight Zone*. For now, I decided to go along. I was at a point where my perspective on her story was equally balanced between seeing it as science-fiction nonsense and assuming it was real. I was truly at a crossroad and had to make the decision to go along or walk away. I decided to accept the challenge. "I have already decided that I'm stuck and might as well go along for the moment," I said.

"You realize that we cannot force you. It has to be entirely free will on your part."

I was beginning to wonder what else was in store for me. What good would it do if I had a fantastic intellectual capability that matched Jane's intellect but an old body and limited energy to keep up with what they were planning to accomplish?

It's a weird situation you're putting me in, I thought.

"When everything is explained to you, you'll be more comfortable with our plans. In the future, we will function as a unit. Our minds will be connected. You must accept that condition, or we'll fail in this venture."

"Does that mean I'll have no privacy at all?"

"No. I have restrictors that only let me process thoughts related to the success of our mission. If you want me to know what you're thinking outside the mission's objectives, you have to allow me to process those thoughts, and only then will I be able to access them. I cannot intrude on your privacy without your consent. And I'm not an android, for your information. I have feelings and emotions but have ways to control them. That's how we function in my world." *You better tread carefully with that one,* I thought.

More Details

"We can infiltrate any place and not be detected, not even by electronic means. Our assignment is to obtain access to classified weapon installations and physically destroy their capabilities. We're to travel to a number of countries and become acquainted with the current development and progress at weapon research advances. You'll be introduced as a theoretical genius who has all the answers to their most difficult development problems." I had to interrupt her. "Can you kindly explain how I can pull that miracle off without a brain transplant?"

"We'll outline that procedure when Aaron is here," Jane continued, undeterred. "You and I will be connected mentally, and when you explain your latest accomplishments in mathematics and physics fields, you'll convince anyone with your extensive knowledge."

"Does that mean that you do your part, presenting the material?"

"No. But you'll have immediate access to all my scientific knowledge. Look at it as an instantaneous, unlimited data bank at your disposal." Jane was presenting this process as if we were ordering our evening meal in a restaurant—all matter of fact and supremely confident. I had a multitude of doubts.

•••••••••●•••••••••

"Our plan is to visit Oxford University in England on our first stop to a number of institutions on your planet. You'll be a guest lecturer for some weeks in their theoretical physics departments and will astonish them with your expertise. We'll make a one week stop at Cambridge University in England and follow that by a short stopover at the Large Hadron Collider (LHC) facility in Switzerland. That will be followed by a similar visit to a nuclear installation in Afghanistan. After your lectures, the Oxford recommendations will be outstanding, and your arrival will be eagerly awaited everywhere else. Afghanistan already has an extensive arsenal of nuclear weapons, but we're not concerned about them. What we do intend to stop is proliferation of those weapons by other nations who have no peaceful intentions. Terrorism in your world is a major concern to us. You may be aware that one of Afghanistan's scientists supplied the details of nuclear bomb manufacturing to Middle Eastern nations and North Korea. The distribution of these design details and research advancements will be stopped through our intervention."

"How do you plan to make me an instant expert in physics and a mathematical prodigy? The complexities of these subjects are so far out that I could not fathom them, even if they were explained in layman's terms."

"Well, that's why your dormant brain capacity will be activated," Jane said.

Cloned

"Jane, I have a question for you. How do you plan to explain my foreign travels to my family and friends, not to mention my sudden appearance at famous universities and nuclear facilities?" I thought I had her here with a problem that could not be resolved and which would derail this crazy idea about my involvement.

"Oh, that has been carefully thought out. We'll clone you, but it will not be an exact copy. It will be a replica, except for your facial features. You can pick anyone and have his looks, say at age thirty-five. That way, you can hide your departure from family and friends in the United States and still have the qualities we require for our tasks that lay ahead. Additionally, you'll have a decision to make about whether you want to have only a facial change or also a new physique. Either way, your own mind will not be affected by the modifications and will function seamlessly with the complements that we'll add. If you wish, you can now decide whose characteristics you want to assume."

"You know, I don't want to insult you but you should be locked up. You're crazy, and I don't believe a word you're saying anymore. Why don't you take your monitor and leave me alone. I don't want my brain manipulated and don't need an extra body. This is all nuts."

She was not even remotely upset by my outburst. "I'll now contact Aaron to have him explain the process."

Before I even had a chance to object, he appeared in the room.

"We're not surprised that you don't want to be duplicated," he said. "I agree with you that it stretches the boundaries of common sense and beliefs, but it's absolutely necessary to hide your disappearance when we're traveling. With your permission, I'll now give you proof that this will be painless and may even be adventurous for you."

"How and where are you planning to perform this duplication? Do I have to go to a laboratory somewhere? I'm sorry, but I can't believe these weird procedures anymore."

"Just tell me that you're ready, and I think you'll be convinced that we're not speaking in riddles. Just say okay."

This whole crock of an affair was getting me annoyed, and I decided to get this over with. "Okay," I yelled out loud and waited.

"I'll have to momentarily attach something to your arm. It will be painless and will take a few minutes," said Aaron.

Both of them were standing next to me, and all I sensed was Jane's proximity. *Is she trying to distract me?*

"Have you made a decision about how you want to look and whether you also want a new exterior?"

Well, I thought, *what am I going to do with a new face and an old body? I might as well go all the way.*

"Yes, I don't want to have a new face with an old body."

"This is irreversible. Are you absolutely sure?"

"Yes, I'm positive, and I want to look like my brother Wil."

"Okay. That's a great choice. Here we go."

I felt nothing and looked triumphantly at both of them. "I knew this was a lot of bull, and I'm not surprised that nothing happened."

"Well," Aaron said. "Go to your bathroom and tell me what you think."

I could not contain my astonishment when I opened the bathroom door. There was my brother Wil looking at me in the mirror. The reflection had the same size frame as I did, except he had Wil's features—a 100 percent copy of how I remembered him. When I recovered from the shock and went back to the living room, I found

Jane and her companion waiting for me, beaming. My old self was standing next to them.

"I hope you're now sufficiently convinced that we're serious about our intentions. Since there are now two of you, it will be prudent to decide how to refer to each of you. How about you, the original, will be Eddie, and your duplicate will be Wil? That should eliminate confusion in the future," said Aaron.

"Agreed," we both said simultaneously. It was funny to me, since we responded the same way. The copy was a copy all right.

"I hope you're not upset. We can duplicate any animate or inanimate object, and we had to demonstrate our abilities in this area. We had to prove the seriousness of our intentions. Why don't you two shake hands, and then we'll continue with the process."

"How complete is my duplicate of Wil? Did I receive his memories?"

"No, the similarity is presently only in the physique and facial features. We have some options for you regarding Wil's moral makeup but will defer those for the moment. In the future you, Wil, will travel with us, while Eddie stays home and interacts as usual with family and friends."

When I stepped out of the fog that was obscuring my sensibility and shook hands with myself; we did not self-destruct as I had expected. Sort of like matter and antimatter. It just felt like another, familiar person. It was strange.

"We'll now ask Eddie to leave the room, while we indoctrinate and prepare Wil for our future travels. We don't want Eddie to be cognizant of any of our plans, in case he's approached by investigative agencies. It is unlikely that any of this will ever be uncovered, but we cannot afford to take chances."

As he left the room, Aaron said that they would prefer not to be referred to as "aliens."

I had thought of them along those lines. "How do you know that I characterized both of you that way? I never uttered that word."

"I had to access to your mind during the cloning procedure, I'm sorry," said Jane.

"That is not what you promised me. You said you needed my consent for allowing access."

"I did, and I'm sorry. In the future I'll refrain from reading your thoughts if you haven't given me permission, but this was an exceptionally critical phase and I had to ascertain that you were capable of tolerating the changes to your body. It will not happen anymore," she said.

I give up, I thought. *They can do whatever they want.*

"Don't give up. Just be nice," she said.

"Let's change the subject. What would you like me to call you?" I asked Aaron.

"Visitor would be more appropriate."

I apologized, and they nodded and smiled.

Preparations

"We'll now outline how we intend to proceed during our university visits. It's by no means going to be an easy undertaking, and we'll encounter some formidable obstacles in the future. The question is, are you ready? Jane and I are prepared for any eventualities, and we can start when you're sufficiently comfortable to proceed."

What could I say? I now had a backup body, just in case the original got damaged in this adventure, and the assurance of our visitors somehow convinced me that this was important and essential. "Okay, I'm ready."

"You won't regret your decision," Aaron said.

"Before we proceed, I have to confess something to you. We obtained your brother Wil's DNA many years ago in preparation for the events to come and have carefully preserved it. We expected that you would want to emulate him."

"It was my idea," said Jane.

"I'm glad you decided on that," I responded.

"We processed and copied all physical characteristics from the DNA, including the facial details. We've also extracted the elements associated with his moral characteristics. We assumed that transferring those to you would give you some stability when you acquired his identity. We've based all of this on the knowledge that he has been your favorite brother. And, by the way, we acquired his DNA from a beer bottle that he used to drink from when he entertained you and your mother on Saturdays with his humorous stories."

I remembered those days well and had even described them in my autobiography. Wil's pleasant personality and his ability to put a light, funny slant on everything he told us, had always made Saturdays the high point of my week. I was glad to have received part of his DNA, even though I questioned the veracity of all the happenings in the last forty-eight hours.

"Okay," I said to Aaron. "Do what you have to do."

"Let me explain what is about to follow. We're going to fuse the dormant regions of your mind with Jane's mental presence. You'll have a symbiotic relationship with her at all times. She can influence your decision making but cannot direct your actions toward anything that is contrary to your moral makeup. In the future, all your decisions have to be completely voluntary. Do you understand and agree?"

"Agreed. Start filling my empty mind."

"The equipment we use is from our dimension, and you cannot see it. I'll describe to you what the procedure is, and you can ask questions at any time. You'll feel a slight tingling on your forehead but will not experience pain. As you probably know, the brain has no pain receptors, and you'll have no discomfort. We'll first install a theoretical foundation layer in the previously dormant, rational region of your mind and let that become functional by interacting with your present mental abilities. It'll take a few days before interactions between unaltered and altered regions become fully integrated. If you have any questions, you should pose them now. Once we start this process, it will be irrevocable."

I felt no discomfort during the mind-blowing procedure and actually felt relaxed. Maybe I was getting comfortable with living this dream.

Jane said that it had taken a half hour when we finished. "You can relax."

"If you don't mind, I would like assurance that the interfacing device with our world wasn't damaged during the flight, when you transported it. Would you mind fetching the monitor for me?" Aaron was clearly concerned about his old display and wanted to check its operation.

I retrieved it from my basement, and he placed it on the table in front of us. When he touched the front, it lit up and made a slight buzzing sound, but that was all.

"You cared well for it," he said.

"Why were you concerned about damage? Will we need this in the future?" I asked.

"This is absolutely essential to completing our mission. Soon you'll see for yourself what a powerful instrument this is."

Modifications

"I think I'm now entitled to an explanation about my part in this exercise. How can I possibly present myself as a formidable expert in fields where I can barely grasp the meaning? The first question asked of me will make me stumble into oblivion."

"Not true," Aaron responded. "You're overlooking the presence of Jane in your mind. Any questions posed to you, no matter how complex, will be processed by her and their answers instantly related to you. We will always ensure that your responses are oblique, pointing in the right direction without providing exact answers or solutions. There exists no question that can be posed that Jane can't answer."

"Aren't you happy that our brains are joined?" she said teasingly.

"Only a little," I responded.

"Our advances in the fields of mathematics and physics would increase the knowledge of your world's weapons researchers, and we cannot risk that. It would escalate the dangers of the armed forces developing even more destructive capabilities, and that is exactly what we plan to prevent," Aaron said. "It's still not clear to me why you selected me for this scientific enterprise. There are plenty of university students in Holland who would have qualified. What is so special about me?"

"As we've told you, you're more special than you realize, and we were impressed by the ways you overcame obstacles in your life. We know what we're doing. With your presentations at universities, you'll be able to whet the appetite of the scientific community, especially since you'll be presented as the foremost expert in fields where their theorists are presently struggling with formidable barriers. Your allusion to solutions, without going into details, will trigger tremendous excitement and will result in a flood of invitations by development laboratories and universities."

"I have no choice but to take your word for it. It just sounds far-fetched to me."

"We have sensed that, and you'll need time to digest the events of the last few days. We'll postpone the next session until you're comfortable with your new self. We don't tire, but we know that you need your rest," Aaron said.

"Are you satisfied with our explanations?" Jane asked with a smile.

"It will do for now, but I have many more questions."

"Okay then. You should take a walk outside with Jane to show your neighbors that you're entertaining visitors." Wow, they seemed to think of everything.

Contact

A half hour later, Jane and I were on our way. My area is sparsely populated, with the majority of houses closed for the winter. When my wife and I purchased the property, we had been the second lot to be occupied, and slowly the remaining acreages had been built on. Many of the owners treated their homes as vacation places, and the result was a quiet neighborhood. When we left my driveway, Jane asked me how I wanted to handle the situation. "Are we an intimate couple or just acquaintances?"

She seemed to have the ability to throw me off with her questions. I figured ignoring her was the proper response. That was apparently not the case in her mind. "I know what you're thinking, and I have no objection to being physically close to you," she said. With that, she hooked her arm through mine, and we were on our way. After a while she asked, "Does it bother you to have me by your side?"

"No, I like it," was all I could utter.

It was disturbing and pleasant at the same time. I still had remnants of my seventy-year-old mind in operation, but Wil's thirty-five-year-old DNA was starting to take effect. It felt similar to when I had met my wife for the first time and to my encounters with the young women in the Far East, when I was in the Dutch merchant marine. There was a definite attraction. My feelings for Jane had slowly increased, but at the same time, the strangeness of the situation put the brakes on for me. I still wasn't convinced whether she was playing games and would ridicule me if I confessed that I felt attracted to her. If this situation was an indication of what I could expect when we were together 24-7, I was in for a rough time.

We walked for about an hour, during which time many cars passed us. I assumed we would come across as visitors living with Eddie in his home, and to those people, Jane and I were probably an item.

My confusion appeared to be unimportant to her. I thought it had been amusing to her, as I had noticed a mild snickering when she hooked her arm through mine. It was probably just a game to her.

When we got back, Aaron had disappeared again, and Jane and I were alone, downstairs. There were three bedrooms in my house, and I assumed that each of us would occupy a separate room. Eddie was upstairs looking at television, and he barely reacted to our return. He only yelled to inquire how the walk had been. He was obviously better adjusted to this situation than I was.

"Would you like to go upstairs and watch TV?" I asked Jane.

"No, I'll be perfectly content in my room. Just tell me which one I should occupy."

"She can have the room on the left, at the end of the hall," said Eddie when I asked him.

As she left, I realized that we'd never discussed having dinner. Now what to do?

"Do you want me to call you when we're ready to eat?" I yelled in the direction of her bedroom.

"No thanks. I'll get my nutrition from my own world, and you wouldn't like it if you observed it."

Okay I thought. *Remember—they are from somewhere else and very different. Don't get attached to this one*, I warned myself, even though I was aware I had already entered that slippery slope.

Eddie and I looked at TV for a few hours, and I thought that we had almost interacted as brothers. I wasn't sure if he felt the same connection as I did and decided to ask.

"What do you think of all this craziness?"

"Well, you're the stuckee and will suffer the consequences. I'm sorry I agreed to this. I'm happy to go on with my seventy-year-old existence. Who knows what lies in store for you, traveling with these two characters?"

The irony of this situation did not escape me. He'd agreed to do this, and I was the victim. He acted as if he had totally accepted the situation. *Could they have influenced him to agree with this scheme?* I wondered. His attitude bothered me.

Super Intelligence

The next morning when I woke up, Jane was standing in my bedroom smiling broadly at me.

"Well, I must say that you're not the bashful type," I said half-jokingly and somewhat annoyed.

"We're not to have any secrets for each other, so get used to it. I know all aspects of you, and there is nothing you have to hide from me. We're basically one—remember?"

Well, if that is her opinion it's not open to interpretation, I thought. "Yeah, but I assumed it would not include infringing on my privacy."

"If we're of one mind, you should have nothing to hide; that's my position."

"I'm not invading your privacy and you shouldn't mine," I said angrily. "Does Aaron agree with your position on this matter?"

"Yes, and you can ask him yourself. He's waiting for us in the living room."

I decided it was a lost cause. She'd made up her mind about our interactions, and in reality, it did not bother me a great deal. It could spice up this business a bit. Nevertheless, it was annoying that I had no privacy anymore. It showed what I could expect from her. As I was getting dressed, I realized that her behavior had stressed me out, and I was winding myself up. I had to discuss this with Aaron.

Surprisingly, he appeared to be ready for me when I entered the living room.

"Ready for the next phase?" he asked.

"No, not exactly. Jane displayed a total disregard for my feelings just now, and this has to be cleared up before I agree to anything else."

"I know. She's already conveyed your reaction to me, and I told her to tone down the physical interactions between the two of you. She can't help it since this is her first encounter with your species, and she's still learning."

"What do you mean? She's still in the bedroom."

"We connect via telepathy because we find your oral communications clumsy. We just adapted to your voice method for interacting with your world. Jane has done a better job than I have in getting used to your speech and vocal sounds. I'm not fond of it. Maybe in time you can adapt to our way. You'll prefer it, I guarantee."

As if by a signal from him, Jane appeared and acted as if nothing had happened in the bedroom.

"Do you feel that you're ready for the next phase? It will be mildly uncomfortable but will open up a new existence for you by giving you mental capacities that are far superior to those of anyone else in your world," Jane said.

I had accepted that exaggeration was not part of my visitors' methods and just braced myself for the next mind-altering experience. They placed their invisible dimension devices on my head, and I felt a light weight, barely noticeable. The sensation was different than when they cloned me, and Aaron explained why that was the case.

"Jane will be connected to you in parallel, and your minds will be fused into a single unit. You'll receive her full intellectual capability, and that will allow you to interact with any physicist or mathematician on your planet. You'll actually be able to converse with Jane directly on her level when this process is completed."

"You mean I'll be as smart as she is?"

"Only on a scientific level," she responded with her special smile.

"Lay off with the bantering," said Aaron.

"We've never transferred this much capacity into another species, and you must inform us immediately if you have reactions or discomfort. We prefer to transfer the complete amount in a single exchange, but if necessary, it can be spread over a number of sessions."

"So far, all I feel is a little pressure on top of my skull and some heat, nothing bad."

In reality, I was very tense and hoped that the transfer would be successful and speedy. The idea of stretching this over multiple sessions did not appeal to me.

I lost all interaction with the environment and drifted into nowhere. Reams of formulas were speeding by, and I was able to recognize and interpret the significance and subjects associated with the data. Most surprisingly, I accepted the fact that I could easily comprehend this material. I became aware of the completion of the process when the weight was removed from my head.

"We assume that this transfer was successful, but we would like your opinion about a breakthrough solution to a difficult problem that was posted in one of the foremost mathematical proceedings in the United States."

Aaron produced the monitor, and it was displaying the solution. It showed me a set of equations that were published in an impressive-looking journal. I looked at the equations for a few minutes and concluded that the proof was correct, but lengthy and elaborate. Investigating the solution had been surprisingly easy for me, and I explained to Jane what my opinion of the validity of the proof was. "The proof is elegant, but I have a simpler solution."

"Show me," she said. "Verbalize the changes you propose. I'll follow you as you work your way through."

I explained my simplification, and she nodded approvingly. I had passed the test.

"Now that you have the necessary smarts, we'll start planning your first visit, which will be to Oxford University in England. Oxford has an excellent theoretical physics department, and you shouldn't have trouble impressing the faculty with your expertise."

Trial by Fire

We stayed with Eddie for another week, and daily activities became repetitive. Jane drilled me every day to make me comfortable with deflecting probing questions about my current research. They expected skeptical audiences and introduced me to the art of responding to questions with "fog balls."

The first time they used this term, I reacted with a chuckle, but got serious pretty quickly when they explained the method behind it.

"You'll have to expect aggressive questions, because Aaron will alert the newspapers prior to our arrival. Controversial breakthroughs in science are always countered in conferences with questions of how, why, and when. British physics and mathematics conferences are especially known for rambunctious encounters between the presenter and the audience."

I guess they're telling me I'm in for it.

"Yes, you are, but you can do it," said Jane.

"In particular, you'll have to explain the answers to two questions In vague language. You should use the 'classified' reason for not detailing solutions to those questions. You can't present the actual proofs of our supposed discoveries at any time."

"How will I know what to withhold?" I was getting uneasy.

"Some of the material you present defines the origin of the universe and the big bang riddle versus dark energy. In our world, we've solved these mysteries millennia ago, but your scientific community isn't ready for a revelation of the mathematical solutions to these vexing problems," Jane explained.

"How am I supposed to make my presentation palatable to the scientists?"

"It will be challenging to give rational answers to the audience's questions without presenting concrete discoveries, but keep in mind, I'm right with you. I'll assist you in formulating vague answers. The first session is always most difficult, but as your confidence increases and your skin thickens, you'll become acclimated. Just have confidence in me."

I must have looked skeptical, because she stopped explaining.

"You're not convinced, are you?" Aaron asked.

"No. I don't see how I can pull this off."

"For now, you'll have no choice but to assume that this can be done by you and Jane. Let her continue outlining how you should present our solutions to the scientists and then take it from there. It's particularly important that you explain that we're close to proving mathematically the answers to questions that will disrupt the scientific community and will seriously affect the world's major nuclear powers," Aaron said.

"We expect a tremendous backlash after your first conference presentation from the scientific world, newspapers, and religious leaders," was Jane's way of relaxing me.

"Well, that's great news to give me, prior to being thrown in the lion's den. You certainly have different ways of putting me at ease."

"This should be enough for one day. Tomorrow we'll continue. Jane will stay with you and answer any questions you have. We'll pick it up when you don't feel so overloaded."

"How do you know how I feel?"

"Jane conveyed it to me," Aaron said with a smile.

"Great. Now I have two psychologists analyzing me. I have thought about allowing Jane to be fully connected to me and I think she should have complete access to my thoughts. I may be asking for trouble but at this time it increases my confidence to present the material, knowing she can gauge my feelings."

"That's a great decision. Are you nervous about having to address the scientific community?" Jane asked.

"What do you think? I've made presentations during my working days, but this scope is somewhat larger than what I'm used to. I'm not impressed by my level of confidence."

"With me in proximity, you'll have no problems. Believe me. Go to bed and accept that we know you can handle these meetings successfully." She smiled and went to her room.

I retreated into my bedroom. I did not sleep well.

We had a few days to prepare me for my important first exposure to the international science world. If I blew this, it would be unlikely I would recover. I had to perform, and I knew it.

·······•·······

Aaron made sure our paperwork was in order for our trip to the English Isles, and even my passport looked believable. The picture was not as bad as my motor vehicle bureau one. And I felt certain that we would not be challenged by customs, with all the hoopla I expected upon our arrival.

We landed at Heathrow Airport and were greeted by banks of reporters from major newspapers and magazines in the country. "Thanks a lot," I managed to say to Aaron as we walked into the arrival hall. It was pandemonium. A section of the hall was roped off, and I was informed that it was expected of me to give a brief outline of my visit to Oxford.

"Keep it short and general," Jane told me, but I couldn't see how I'd get away with that. The welcoming committee was headed by the president of the university, and even the minister of Science and Technology was present. I felt like a cornered rat with a large number of cats preparing to rip me apart.

"Tell them that you feel honored by the welcoming committee and take it from there," I heard Jane say. "Just wing it."

I started by thanking the dignitaries and told them that it was unusual to see such interest in science. "I do hope that your expectations have not been blown out of proportion. I know some of my research may be construed as heresy and may upset your religious communities. Many of you will defend the validity of established theories. My visit to your country will brief but eventful, that I can promise."

There was shouting by reporters, who hurled questions in my direction, but the police officers guided me directly to an exit. A limousine was waiting, and we were on our way to the hotel. Jane was sitting next to me in the back and she whispered, "Good job. I'm proud."

I was surprised. I thought I had blown it.

This whole affair, however short, had given me a taste of what was to come. My two handlers would have to give me ammunition to prevent the academic crowd from tearing me apart.

My Ultimatum

That night I had trouble sleeping, thinking about whole nightmarish process that was unfolding. After hours of lying awake, I made a decision. No matter what, I would hold my ground. I would give a presentation on parallel universe discoveries, dark matter, and the origin of our universe. If they did not agree with this, I would back out of the deal. Jane would have to furnish me with the details. I refused to be humiliated in front of the academic vultures.

After the restless night, I felt like hell, but got up anyway. Under the circumstances, with all my worries, it was useless to attempt to go back to sleep. To my surprise, Jane was waiting for me in the living room with a black coffee, just to my liking. "We have to talk," she said.

"Yeah, what else is new," was my response.

"I know you had a difficult night, and I feel badly for you. We've given you an impossible task, and I'm not even sure I can pull it off. You still don't realize how completely our brains are connected, but I experienced the same anxieties as you did last night. You cannot keep anything from me. If you're going to present details about your research in the three areas you insist on covering, Aaron will need permission from the science council in our dimension."

"What are the chances they'll agree?"

"Aaron is the president of the council, and if he can't convince them, nobody can. We'll have to wait. I informed him of your decision, and he agreed to present our dilemma to the council. Tomorrow we'll get his answer. I'll contact the university and tell them that you're recovering from the strenuous trip and cannot have any visitors today. Go back to bed and relax. You're useless when you're tired and stressed out."

........●..........

The next day, Aaron returned and informed us that the council had decided to let me discuss the three topics, provided Jane's filtering would be activated during my presentation. This was an unknown capability she had. *Could she just disable my vocal cords while I was in the middle of presenting my research status?*

"What does Jane's intervention mean?"

"One simple method would be to disable the PA system or kill power to the building, but that's a little brute force."

"So how do I proceed?"

"The council voted to approve your demands but wants a safeguard in case you inadvertently stray into an area that should not, at this time, be revealed. Your world is simply not ready for some of these technological breakthroughs. They also want Jane and me to be present during the presentation. It's deemed to be prudent to introduce us to the world as your two colleagues who have been actively involved in the research. That way, after the presentation, questions can be addressed to us as a team. That'll make it easier for you and should spread questions among our group. We have to be careful with hyperbole. The members in this audience have been at the forefront with their own research and will not let us get away with unsupported theories or responses."

"Well, good luck to us. I think we'll need it," I responded.

My two team members seemed to be amused and relaxed about my reaction. I just wondered how badly we would be slaughtered during this conference with all the exposure and expectations that had been aroused.

The Conference

Two days later, we were under the gun. This university is well endowed and their auditorium was enormous. Not a single seat was vacant. I estimated its capacity was a thousand people. A number of seats at the podium were already occupied, and the provost of the institute was beaming in my direction when we entered. Remarkably, I was not nervous. The decision to present my findings as a team had reduced my nervousness to background noise, which I could handle. I was introduced as Dr. William Smither from the University at Leiden in Holland and a foremost researcher in the origin of the universe and dark matter.

After the usual acknowledgements and thanking the university provost for the generous accommodations, I began by introducing my two team members.

Dr. Aaron Zxannaq, premier researcher in the fields of astrophysics and higher-dimensional universes, and Dr. Jane Qzxanq, expert on black holes, dark matter, and strong/weak forces.

"We've collaborated as a team for ten years," I told the audience. "Questions can be addressed to any team member, following the presentation."

"Don't overdo it," Jane whispered.

"Since this audience is a mixture of journalists, students, and members of the scientific community, we'll describe our findings in general terms, rather than detailed scientific discussions. Some solutions may be abbreviated because of classification restrictions. Details will be provided to small working groups, designated by the university."

Aaron had discussed that with the president of the university, and he had agreed. General discussions would be sufficient during the conference.

An unhappy murmur arose from the audience after my statement.

"Four topics we'll discuss are:

* Big bang and the origin of our universe,
* Black holes and matter transfer,
* Parallel universes,
* Dark matter.

I have to stress that we're in the preliminary phases but have made sufficient progress to describe our results thus far. The findings are all theoretical. Our discoveries will correct some current misconceptions and cause objectives at institutions and laboratories to be changed. Let me be more precise."

I decided to pause slightly to give the audience a chance to prepare for what was being delivered.

"First, the origin of our universe was investigated, and our discoveries explained many unresolved questions. We've found that our universe has a companion, a brother/sister configuration. It can also be described as a ping/pong existence."

I inserted another short pause and then continued.

"At the present time, our universe is populated with billions of galaxies, while our sister universe is void of matter. The connections between the two universes are black holes in every galaxy. These black holes absorb matter and reduce it to its basic constituents, transmitting it into a buffer space, which separates the two companion universes. During this transmission, the black holes change normal matter into antimatter. Brother/sister universes always have this opposite matter configuration. The shapes of the two universes are ellipsoid disks, where the furthest galaxies are located along the major axis. The buffer area between them contains the strong force component of dark matter. This prevents the two companion universes from annihilating each other."

I paused again for a minute, which was a mistake. My presentation was having the effect we wanted, but I was getting uncomfortable with the whispering in the audience, which was now noticeable. I was losing control as the arguing became louder. I turned around and looked at Aaron, who was sitting with Jane and the dignitaries. Aaron realized that this was getting disruptive and addressed the audience. "You were informed what our conditions would be when we discussed our current progress. This is not parliament, where shouting is common. Anyone who is incapable of refraining from interfering with the presenter is urged to leave. We will not tolerance this."

Aaron gestured for me to continue, and no more interruptions occurred.

"We've discovered that we're surrounded by a multitude of brother/ sister universes. Many of these have different dimensions than ours. Our universe and multidimensional ones cannot interact. This is prevented by the buffering of the strong force. Wormholes between adjacent universes exist and have been uncovered by us. At the moment, they're just theoretical. When we're satisfied that our conclusions are sound, we'll present them to the community, later this year."

I paused again, fully expecting another rowdy outburst, but the audience was just looking expectedly at me. Aaron's warning had been effective.

I felt more confident and continued. "We've extensively investigated dark matter and have proof that it consists of different configurations."

"Be careful here; you can't give us away," whispered Jane without uttering a sound. Somehow, she planted her concern directly into my conscience.

I heeded her warning but couldn't understand how she was able to accomplish this from fifteen feet away. I knew what she meant, but her words had not reached me through the air. I also realized that not all of their interactions with me had been explained. I indicated to her that I understood with a hand gesture and continued with the next topic.

"There are two types of dark matter—strong and weak energy. We've discovered that the strong force has two functions. This force separates multidimensional universes from merging with ours, and it separates the sister/brother universes. The weak force interacts with gravity."

I inserted another pause to let the audience absorb the information.

"The buffer zone separation force is immensely powerful. Current fusion results, produced on earth, are baby steps compared to the incredible energy potential present in this force. It, unfortunately, could lead to the development of even more destructive devices than those we already have—devices that could physically annihilate our planet. We have struggled with this discovery, and it has caused me many sleepless nights. The destructive potential is so great that we have decided not to publish the results."

This was evidently disturbing to the audience, and a noticeable murmur emanated from the auditorium. I gave them a few minutes to digest this unexpected news and continued.

"The third topic, which is close to my heart, is the presently accepted big bang theory. With our discovery of the adjacent parallel universes, we have concluded that the results produced by Einstein's general relatively theory are correct, up to the point of where the singularity occurs. The singularity is, in reality, a massive black hole that pulls in the galaxies from the existing universe and shunts them into the receiving buffer void. Nothing is lost, and nothing is gained. Instead, immense energy is released, which is absorbed by the strong dark matter force. This is the major component produced during the annihilation process by a black hole. If the (LHC) in Switzerland were able to produce a small black hole, it would verify our theory and produce the strong component of dark matter."

I decided to give them another minute to think about the dark matter revelation and continued after the whispering in the audience had subsided.

"The black hole transfer process ejects matter into the receiving sister universe buffer queue space. This process continues until equilibrium is reached between the strong force component and the total mass of matter in the buffer queue. At that moment, an ultra massive black hole forms, which releases the queue matter into the sister universe."

More whispering from the audience was noticeable.

"This ultra massive black hole in the buffer space, which can overcome the queue separating force, is estimated by us to have a mass on the order of a hundred billion of our sun's mass, and its energy is sufficient to overcome the barrier force. When that happens, the matter is released from the buffer space into the sister's universe void, where it eventually becomes a maximally occupied entity. This process is currently known as the big bang. In the previously void sister universe, regular black holes form, and the process repeats itself. The ultra massive black hole formation repeats about every fifteen billion years."

I was done with my presentation and waited for a response from the audience. There were an unexpectedly low number of questions. It was as if everyone had been stunned by our concepts. The few questions asked were answered by Jane, and we were done. I had survived.

That night, the tabloids had a feast:

"Dutch team of scientists explains origin of the universe."

"We're surrounded by multi dimensional universes, with probably alien populations."

"Why are the Dutch scientists unwilling to divulge the enormous energy source? Future weapons?"

"What is their next move? Selling it to the highest bidder?"

"This reaction was exactly what we'd hoped for," said Aaron.

"It gives us the exposure we need to be invited to other venues and, ultimately, to attain our goal."

"You did great," was Jane's opinion.

"Let's talk about our goals for a minute. What exactly is the purpose of all this? You have never made that clear to me," I responded.

"It's still too early to explain what our goal is. I expect to see many visitors who will be interested in our findings. In due time, you'll be told exactly why we decided to have this charade. For now, just enjoy yourself."

The US Contingent

T he auditorium slowly emptied. After shaking hands with the university dignitaries, we exited the place. In the hallway, we were approached by four impeccably dressed individuals. Two were military. "Dr. Smither, may we have a word with you?"

"Well sure. Did you like the presentation?"

"That happens to be why we would like to have a word with you. We have a conference room reserved, where we'll have privacy."

"I have no objections, but I want my team to be present for this."

"That's fine with us," he said, and we walked down the hall to a room that had a guard posted outside. "These peoples are up to no good. You have to watch how you respond," whispered Jane, but again not via voice. As we were seated, one of the military guys introduced the visitors. "We're members of the US intelligence community and are here on our president's orders," he said. His sharp eyes and clipping tone, along with the intimidating posture of his companions made it clear the meeting was intended to convince us to reveal our research results to them. "I'm Colonel Jack Jones, representing the US Army Intelligence Corps," he continued. "Next to me is Guy Friedrich, with the CIA. To my right is Fred Johnson. He's a member of the newly created cyber warfare organization. And last is Sally Leifer. She's with the FBI. We have been instructed to invite you to the United States to brief our military about your research findings and share your conclusions with our development teams."

"They want you to make bombs for them," Jane whispered. "You have to refuse."

"I'm sorry, but I'm not prepared to share that information with anyone right now. It is too preliminary. When I'm ready to publish my findings, you'll be notified through the established scientific channels."

"We expected you to react this way but must warn you. This is regarded as a national security situation by the highest US authorities, and we expect you to comply." I had never reacted well to ultimatums, and this started to annoy me. "I'm a Dutch citizen, and you cannot force me to accompany you to the United States. However, I have no objection to spending some time in your country at your expense. But there's an outstanding possibility that I'll develop amnesia on the flight across. I cannot guarantee that I'll remember anything. This has happened to me before when I was forced to comply with unreasonable demands."

"Well done," Jane related. "This conversation stays in this room, understood." Yes Sir, was my sarcastic response.

Jane's Emotions

We spent three more weeks at Oxford, and I had no presentations to make. The tumult our conference had caused was plastered all over the major newspapers with sensational headlines. It was somewhat disturbing to me, since all the attention had instantly raised me to celebrity status at the university. In particular, two female postdoctoral students paid a lot of attention to me, which appeared to bother Jane a great deal. It started with a few snide remarks Jane made in passing about the scatterbrains who were hanging around me when I was having talks with the staff. Then she became outright nasty with her comments. First, I thought it was best to ignore her. But when Aaron asked me if I knew what was bothering her I decided to confront her. After breakfast, I asked her to take a walk with me. "Why are you so nasty lately?" I asked her.

"I don't know. I can't help it. I've never had the urge to be confrontational with anyone, and now I can't stand seeing you talk with those two women."

"Would you like my opinion?"

"Yes, very much so, since it bothers me that I can't stop behaving this way."

"Well, your method of fusing our brains has someway rebounded into yours, and you're now the owner of some human emotions. You're jealous, dear."

"That's not possible. I have never heard of anything like this happening."

"Well, how many fusing experiments have you witnessed?"

"None, but my training had always indicated that it's not possible."

"There you go; practical experience is always best. Welcome to the human existence. Now the question you should ask yourself is how you'll react toward me in the future. We're frequently in close proximity, and you may start experiencing feelings that will be confusing and difficult to control. I suggest that you explain to Aaron what has happened. You'd better hope he has a solution. And, by the way, I'm having feelings for you that I have difficulty suppressing. This fusion experiment may turn out to have unexpected side effects for both of us."

The following morning, Jane told me to take another walk with her.

"I told Aaron what's happening to me, and he's as confounded as I am. He's never heard of such a possibility either. But then, this was the first time a human brain was fused with one of us. He's asked members of the council, and they did not have an explanation. He told me that visitors from our dimension have routinely married members of your race, but none of those alignments involved brain fusions. The only problem that those married couples encountered were that the female visitors could not conceive children. The male visitors had no difficulties whatsoever. It must be an anomaly, which will probably be discussed among our scientist. I think this situation may be unique, and we'll have to live with it."

"Live with it in what way? Your behavior in the past has already disrupted my existence, so I don't feel sorry for you at all. You showed up out of nowhere and practically forced me into cohabitation with you. Even though you may have done it unwittingly, you've stirred my emotions in ways that I was totally unprepared for. Therefore, if this situation is bothersome to you, I frankly couldn't care less. It bothers me a great deal too."

"Well, it's confusing to me and it disturbs me. It may affect my interactions with you in the future," she replied.

"I suggest you keep your distance, both physically and emotionally. Your proximity has been an issue ever since you waltzed into my life. My suggestion is that you keep your quarters at night in your dimension. Six degrees of separation may do us some good," I said.

"What are you talking about? It is not six degrees at all," she responded.

"I'm just testing your ability to process humor. I don't think you'll ever acquire that skill."

"You're getting nasty lately. Why?" She sounded as if my comment had hit a nerve, if she had any.

"You disrupted my life and have thrown me for emotional loops. You're insensitive about other people's feelings. And my reaction surprises you? Get a life. Let your physiologists at home analyze this situation for you. I suspect they'll have marginal success."

She looked shaken when she disappeared to her own environment.

I had mixed emotions after this outburst. I unfortunately had developed a strong attraction to her that I could not suppress, but I realized that this had to be brought into the open if she was to be living with me.

· · · · · ●●●● ● ●●●●●● · · · ·

The next two weeks, I had a relatively easy time. The technical briefings were done by my team members, and I could enjoy the spectacle from a safe distance. Aaron and Jane told me that it had been difficult to deflect probing questions, and there was skepticism galore during the meetings. I was glad I was off the hook. At night, Jane disappeared, and I enjoyed a quiet existence. She appeared to have accepted that her proximity bothered me.

I had been able to avoid daily contact with the two women who were interested in me. It wasn't that I didn't like their flirting but, rather, that I wanted to avoid getting Jane upset.

We made a one-week stopover at Cambridge University, and Aaron decided we'd had sufficient exposure in England. The Cambridge faculty had obtained the presentation material from Oxford, and I presented it in an abbreviated format. Since the audience was well acquainted with our current research status from Oxford, it was a low-stress meeting for me with few questions. I had become confident in my ability to coexist with foremost experts in theoretical physics and mathematics and felt relaxed during the questioning period. I was learning to deflect probing questions.

Jane adjusted to our normalized situation and appeared to have accepted that we should keep our distance—or so I thought.

The invitations to major European institutions appeared the day after the last Cambridge presentation, and Aaron informed me that the Swiss (LHC) was at the top of the list. "If we can impress the LHC scientists, we'll have guaranteed open invitations to the rest of the world. We're on track," he told me.

"We're on track to what? When are you going to tell me what the purpose of this exercise is?"

"Be patient a little longer. All will be revealed soon."

"I sure hope so. I feel that I'm just being used."

"When we're done here, we'll go to Switzerland to visit the LHC, and there I'll outline our plan."

We left Cambridge, and I wondered how successful I had been in my role. I decided to corner Aaron.

"Yes, our presentations have aroused tremendous interest in our research. You've provided the scientific world with sufficient data to get them excited about our findings. My worry was that you would cave in under the strain, but you performed flawlessly. Especially Jane is pleased with your performance. It was well above our expectations."

Hallelujah. This I had not expected. As long as she's only pleased with my technical performance, I'll be happy. Hope she stays out of the emotional section of our shared minds.

"Now, when we get to the LHC, we have to be careful what we present. These people are very sharp and have made giant strides lately. In particular, the dark matter and black hole part of your presentation has drawn their interest. We'll have to formulate our answers carefully."

I didn't expect much else.

Telepathy

The nonverbal communications Jane and Aaron had with each other increasingly began to bother me. It left me wondering what they were conspiring. This came to a head when we were discussing possible ramifications of the LHC presentation we had planned, and they totally excluded me from their conversation. They were nodding and agreeing, without including me. My short temper got the best of me, and I told Aaron to "lay off" with the private discussions and include me.

"Sorry, but we find it a strain to converse via voice."

"Well, isn't it about time you give me the ability to use telepathy?"

"It's not that we don't want to. Rather, it's that we can't predict the outcome."

"What does that mean? Is it dangerous?"

"It requires us to modify your RNA and DNA, and that has never been done."

"Well, you screwed enough with my body so far. Why not go all the way?"

"This may pose a significant risk to you, and I need to clear this with the council."

"Look, I have a spare body at home, and if you blow this experiment, it will be your loss. I'll just return to my restful existence in the United

States. From now on, I don't want to be left out of conversations between you two, and I have to insist on the procedure."

Noting that I was determined, Aaron nodded and disappeared.

"You're becoming a little cocky," Jane said. "Don't let your recent success go to your head."

"It has nothing to do with that. I still feel like a puppet that is being controlled by you, and it gives me agita. I've also made up my mind that I will not comply with unreasonable demands anymore. If you guys don't like it, find another victim."

"Calm down and have a glass of wine with me. It will relax you," she said.

"No thanks. Just leave me alone. And don't hang around, unless you need me for the job."

She looked disturbed when she disappeared.

·········●·········

They both appeared a few hours later and looked worried.

"You've given us no alternative," Aaron said. "We'll attempt to give you the ability to communicate on our level. But before we start the procedure, I have to explain to you what has to be changed in your DNA and RNA structures. I had a meeting with our best physiologists, and none could predict the outcome. Nobody was prepared to guarantee the consequences when RNA structures are altered in a human. Some called it a crapshoot."

"At this point, it makes little difference to me how risky it is," I told them. "I don't want to be excluded anymore in the future, and I insist that you give me the telepathic ability."

"Okay, but let me explain why it's difficult. Your DNA is a helix, which is the same configuration as ours. The difference is that ours is more complex and contains more elements. To give you the increased abilities, we only have to append portions of our DNA structure to yours. That's a low-risk procedure."

"So what's the big deal then?"

"Stop interrupting and listen," Aaron said.

"This is an extremely dangerous procedure; I may lose you," injected Jane.

"That's no big deal. You can just start over with another candidate walking the earth."

I was not prepared for Jane's reaction. She burst into tears and disappeared.

"Well, now you've done it," said Aaron. "You're not only jeopardizing our successful completion, but you're also destroying Jane emotionally. Congratulations."

Aaron's biting comment made me realize that I had badly misjudged Jane's and his intentions. They were protecting me from my own stupidity, and I had not recognized it. Jane's reaction bothered me the most. *Why the emotional outburst? Could she have the same strong feelings for me as I have for her?*

"Maybe you're seeing the light," Aaron said. "With all your previous experience with women, as you so eloquently described in your autobiography, you're totally blind, judging Jane's devotion to you. I'm leaving and will be back tomorrow. I suggest you evaluate your position and let us know whether we should proceed."

Aaron left me in disarray, wondering if I was falling in love with Jane. It was a crazy thought—caring for a being from another world. I had suppressed my feelings for Jane, and realism about the probability of us pairing had always been my reasoning. But after this event, I looked at the situation differently. Maybe it could work between Jane and me; it was worth a try. I made up my mind to apologize to her and confess that I love her, irrespective of the consequences.

The feeling my decision left me with was similar to what I had experienced during my merchant marine days with two different women, and the familiarity was both comforting and upsetting. The unknowns were worrisome, especially having experienced the aftereffects of the mind fusing with Jane. Although Jane was already roaming around in my head at will, the effects of telepathy could introduce another unknown. I wondered what I was getting into. The telepathic addition could affect our fused brains in unexpected ways. They didn't know what to expect, and neither did I. "Another great situation you've got me in," as they used to say in the movies.

Jane and Aaron reappeared the next morning. Jane acted distant and avoided my gaze. I was in for it, having to figure out how this woman worked emotionally.

"Have you decided to continue, and do you accept the risks?" said Aaron.

"I've given it considerable thought and decided to do the alteration. If something goes wrong, you can decide what to do with the body."

"That's not funny," Jane said, looking annoyed.

"Well, I'm prepared for anything, so let's get this over with. I have accepted that our adventure may end here, and I'm not dramatic, just realistic."

"Okay then, let me explain one more time how we will alter your DNA and RNA. The RNA structure we have is entirely different than humans have. Ours is a double-stranded helix, similar to DNA, while yours is single-stranded. None of our RNA specialists is prepared to predict the outcome when we fuse part of ours with your RNA. We'll have to append part of our double design to your single structure. Do you understand why we're concerned about the outcome?"

"Yes, and I still want to proceed. If we're to work together as a close-knit group, I want to have the same toolset as you."

"You have brass balls," said Jane. I nearly fell out of my seat, when she said that. "Where did you pick up that kind of language? Women don't normally use that slang."

"I heard it at Oxford, and I have a great memory. It sounded useful.

"Well, now that we got that out of the way," said Aaron, "let me tell you how we'll safeguard the essential parts of your modified body. We'll make copies of your complete DNA and RNA structures, just in case some unexpected anomaly results. That way, we can try to reinstate your unmodified genetics. You can view that as a life insurance policy."

"Would that be up to me?"

"Yes, but you may not be capable of making that decision. You'll have to give Jane permission to make that decision for you."

Now or never. I have to tell her how I feel before they evaporate me." Can you give me a minute alone with Jane?" I asked Aaron.

"Of course. I'll be ready when you are." Aaron left, and I was alone with Jane. "Come here please, and hold my hand," I told her. "Since there is a chance I may not survive this, I have to tell you that I love you."She looked surprised and was ready to respond. "Don't interrupt and let me continue. I gave it a lot of thought last night, and I want you to know how I feel about you. I never expected this to happen, and it pleases and confuses me. If I survive this operation, you can tell me if you think our connection could work. Otherwise, it doesn't matter." She looked at me intently and bent over, kissing me. "Does that answer your question?" she said. "I'll see you in an hour." Aaron appeared, and I was under the knife. "We're reasonably sure that we can reintroduce the stored DNA and RNA if something unexpected happens," Aaron said. "Well, with my new intellectual capabilities, I deal in probabilities. What's the chance of success?"

"I'd say 75 percent, but Jane assumes 100."

"You have no idea how relieved I am."

"Let me know when you're ready."

"I am. Let's get this over with."

The Genetic Modification

―――――――――――――――   ―――――――――――――――

"For this procedure, Jane has agreed to have part of her DNA and RNA copied and transferred to yours. It will not be done in the brain but rather in the spinal cord fluid. Your body will distribute the modifications and change your genetic makeup to mimic parts of ours. It will be painless but will take longer than the initial transfer we did to make you smart." Jane was lying on the table next to me. I felt invisible devices being attached and heard Aaron say that he would hook them up to my lower back. After a few minutes, I noticed a slight vibration on my skin but that was all. "It will take about an hour," I heard Aaron say. I drifted away and lost contact with the environment. When I sensed my surroundings again, I felt Jane lying next to me. She touched my arm and asked, "How do you feel?"

"Are we done yet?" I asked.

"Almost. The dangerous part is done."

"We need about a half hour more to complete this portion. We didn't want to take chances and paused repeatedly to check on your body's acceptance of the changes."

"Okay, just wrap it up. I'm getting restless lying next to you."

"Nonsense, we already have mental contact, and you're enjoying it," she said. For a while, I felt nothing but the vibration, and then slowly the area started to heat up. *It's getting warm*, I thought. To my surprise Aaron responded. "It means we're on track."

"Well you're right. I was picking up your thought also. I'm very relieved we were successful." said Jane. Not via voice, but directly into my brain. The procedure was obviously working. Aaron continued to lay his thoughts directly on me. "We're almost done, so be patient," he transmitted. It was amazing. It all registered in my brain. It came through crystal clear, as if he had spoken the words, and I felt relaxed about hearing them in my mind.

"We're still not done, so relax," Jane relayed to me. "It looks like it will be a success. We may have to take you to our dimension to show you off." I noticed the procedure was complete when the equipment was removed. It had been painless, but I could not say I had been without worries. "This will make it so much easier in the future for us to communicate with each other. You have to understand that there are some restrictions. Nothing can interfere, but distance plays a part. Within fifty feet, it will work. If a room is shielded, like with X-ray procedures at your dentist, you're out of luck. But for our future conferences, it will be enormously helpful to be able to communicate with each other without anyone being aware," Aaron explained. "I'll be leaving to brief my people at home," Aaron added. "They're anxiously waiting to hear how it worked."

The LHC

The Large Hadron Collider visit was next. I knew nothing about the collider, and Jane explained its function to me. "CERN is the European Organization for Nuclear Research. Its offices are in Geneva, Switzerland. That's our next stop. We'll hold our briefings for a week at the offices in Geneva, and then visit the LHC site. We're going to advise them how to produce dark matter, but not in sufficient detail to accomplish it."

"I thought these discussions were off limits?"

"That's true to a degree, but we have to convince them that we've reached a breakthrough in this area."

"That sounds like a formidable task," I said.

"Don't worry about it. Aaron is prepared to carry the ball this time."

"More slang. You're learning fast," I said to Jane.

"If I'm staying with you, I have to learn the ropes," she said, winking.

"They've increased their collider power output lately but are still far from the level that produces even a shadow of a black hole. As you well know from our previous Oxford presentations, a black hole generates dark matter. Our findings have been circulated throughout the academic world, and fog balls won't go over well with these people," said Jane.

"I'm glad I'm not under the gun here," I said to Aaron.

"You and Jane will be the backup in case I flounder," he said with a broad smile.

Man, talk about confidence, I thought.

"You'll get there," Jane responded into my brain. It disoriented me momentarily, and I realized my future interactions with them were irreversibly altered by the telepathic connection I had with them.

Jane now continued with her explanation. "In our world, we used colliders like these millennia ago. I had to access our archives to refresh myself on the initial designs we used and have briefed Aaron. At this time, the Security Council in our world is not concerned about breakthrough progress in Switzerland. Do you find it hard to believe their collider is considered a child's toy by us?" Jane asked.

"I have stopped questioning anything you tell me," I told her.

"I hope that includes believing how I feel about you," she said.

"Yes. That pre-RNA kiss made a believer out of me."

"Stick to the subject," Aaron interjected.

"You'll be introduced as the purely theoretical member of our group, and you'll be on the sidelines. Aaron will do the heavy lifting at the lab and be introduced as the hardware expert. We'll link our minds during his discussions with the lab scientist, and that will allow you to fully comprehend the material. It will be advanced, and our connection will be dynamic. No more of your vocal cord exercises, to my great relief I may add," Jane said.

We flew from Heathrow, England, to Zurich and were met by the expected delegation of government officials, scientist, and journalists. Actually, a larger crowd than had greeted us during the initial exposure we got in England. This time, I was relaxed enough to enjoy the spectacle.

Jane volunteered to handle the logistics of dealing with this crowd. The TV and newspaper representatives were firing many questions in our direction. It was remarkable to me how she remained unflustered, no matter the barrage of screaming reporters, airport engine noise, and security trying to keep the crowd at bay.

It would have been stressful for me to handle this environment. As I was thinking this, she connected with me directly. "That's why I did not want you to do this. Your self-confidence has increased, but these events can be unpredictable, and you need a solid footing to handle any eventualities. You'll get there. Don't worry. Just watch and learn."

Amazing, the confidence this woman has. Will I ever attain her level? I wondered.

"You will, I promise."

Damn, I'm still not used to being connected with you.

"We're of one mind. Get used to it," was her reply.

I thought it would be difficult for Aaron to present the appropriate material without giving away our identities, but he assured me that he had it under control. "What I'll show is enough to get them on the path of new discoveries, but insufficient for dangerous breakthroughs. I'll reveal just enough to get them excited."

I wondered how he would do that.

Then Jane piped in. "You've only scratched the surface of our capabilities. You'll be astonished when we eventually reveal all our knowledge to you."

"Well, your methods are still somewhat foreign to me. I even remember some coercion from you in convincing me of your ways," I said.

"That's not how I remember it," Jane responded, smiling.

It's senseless to argue with her. You might as well accept it.

"Good decision," she inserted in my mind.

· · · · · · ● ● ● ◉ ● ● ● · · · · · ·

The next week was devoted to Aaron briefing the physicist and engineers of the LHC. Aaron decided to limit the size of the meetings to LHC personnel and a small number of academics. The director of the LHC objected to this, but Aaron had been adamant. "I'll only conduct meetings that are manageable," he'd told him. He had no choice but to accept Aaron's decision.

After the first meeting, he told me the reason for keeping the meeting small.

"The amount of questions asked is always proportional to the number of brains that are present. With too many people the encounters would drag out too long, and that is not in our best interest. We're limiting everything to the bare minimum, from feeding them solutions to our time spent here. It will be just enough to make them hungry."

I understood what he meant but thought I would have expressed it somewhat differently.

"Usually, what we say is not open to interpretation," Jane said.

"I give up. You guys are always right, no matter what. Pull my strings and manipulate me any way you want. My opinion doesn't count; I know that much."

She looked at me surprised, as if my reaction was totally unexpected. She looked at Aaron, and he nodded. They excluded me from their conclusion about my attitude, even though I shared Jane's mind.

The next morning, Aaron told me to take a stroll with him. "Geneva has beautiful boulevards, and it is a nice, sunny day," he said.

"I want to talk to you about the reaction you had when Jane and I communicated, and left you out. We have levels of connecting with each other that have to be activated by us. It's like your security system where you have to acquire a 'need to know' for access. It is not that we don't trust you. As we progress in our journey, attempts will be made by governments to obtain our knowledge and expertise. Jane and I cannot be interrogated or held captive, for that matter, because we can transfer into our dimension at will. You, however, cannot. We have to withhold information from you, to keep you safe."

I began to understand. Remembering the US contingent was enough for me to agree with him.

Before I could utter a word, he said.

"Yes, those guys are up to no good, and I expect we'll see them frequently at our meetings."

Aaron was right. Jones, Friedrich, Johnson, and Leifer were hanging around the LHC conferences and attempted to be included in the scientific briefings that Aaron conducted each day. Only his strenuous objections prevented their attendance.

Briefings at the LHC Laboratory

I was instructed to attend but not add to the discussions, unless I was specifically approached. I did not feel excluded and was relaxed about the evolving events. The lab attendance was restricted to twenty-five people, and attendees were selected by LHC management. Aaron introduced Jane and me as team members, and the proceedings were under way. Aaron briefed the audience on our latest research status regarding black holes and dark matter, stressing that all our efforts were purely theoretical. "Please abstain from questioning until I've completed my presentation," he said before getting started.

When he was done, the avalanche of questions commenced.

"Can you be more specific about your black hole discoveries?"

"Our colleagues at Oxford informed us about your dark matter findings."

"How do you know that dark matter has two components?"

The audience members were now arguing among themselves about what topics should be discussed, and Aaron seemed amused about the excitement their own questions had generated. He had a gavel at the lecture stand and pounded with it.

The discussions subsided, and he continued. "We first want to congratulate your teams at this facility for their achievements in discovering new particles. In particular, the Higgs boson was impressive. We've investigated what your facility needs to accomplish to facilitate discovery of additional particles. With the current power output of the LHC at approximately eight TeVs, it was sufficient to discover the Higgs boson. However, our research has shown that more extensive power is required to create miniature black holes (strangelets), in your laboratory environment. He used the TeV abbreviation for Terra electron Volts with this audience because they usually referred to the LHC power requirements that way.

From the stirring in the audience, it was clear to me that they had not expected this kind of information.

"The LHC has to be enlarged, and the beam structure has to be altered. I'll now provide details. Our research indicates that the following minimum adjustments have to be made to the current design to produce an initial, miniature black hole. A minimum power output of one hundred TeVs is required to generate a small black hole. Between the present eight-TeVs output and the necessary expansion to the hundred-TeVs limit, a large number of exotic particles will be discovered, so it should not be construed as a waste if a black hole cannot be produced."

From the murmurs that were reaching me from the audience, it was clear to me that the requirements Aaron described came as a shock.

"To reach the limit that produces a black hole will require enlarging the ring from the current 17 miles to a minimum of 120 miles and doubling the dual beams to a total of four. These are the requirements to produce a black hole. The focusing and simultaneous bombardment of the target material by the four beams has to occur within picoseconds."

"That should give them some sleepless nights," Jane transmitted.

Aaron wasn't done yet. "When a miniature black hole can be reliably produced, the resulting particle analysis will show the composition of dark matter to consist of a weak and a strong entity. The strong component especially requires special attention. It is extremely volatile and cannot be easily, or safely, contained. A miniscule black hole's output of the dark matter strong force can produce more energy than a hundred kilograms on your best fissionable material. I urge the scientific community not to pursue this research. In the wrong hands, it could lead to destruction of our planet."

Wow, how well will this go over with the US contingent?

"Don't worry. No single nation can afford to build a collider large enough to create anything near the necessary capacity," said Jane. "We're just doing this to get into the newspapers tomorrow."

There were heated discussions in the audience after Aaron had completed his presentation, and he answered a number of questions with as much vagueness as he could muster. I was glad I was not involved.

Aftermath

As we assumed, the newspapers had a field day. A person in the audience had informed the press about our meeting with the LHC community, and the guessing and outlandish interpretations were outstanding fodder for publication:

"End of the world predictions"

"LHC on steroids"

"Many trillions necessary to build a larger LHC"

"Bigger bombs in the future?"

When my two companions saw how the papers had blown everything out of proportion, they were pleased.

"This is exactly what we hoped for," said Jane.

I still couldn't figure out the purpose of riling everybody up about our research discoveries and was getting annoyed with my companions. "Don't you two think it is about time to fill me in on the purpose of your visit to our backward little planet?"

"Very soon we'll tell you" said Aaron.

"Sorry, but that won't fly anymore. I'm stumbling in the dark here, and I have no idea why I agreed to cooperate. I'm upset and fed up."

"Okay, when we complete this stop, we will fill you in. The presence of the US contingent has us concerned, and we don't want to risk exposing ourselves."

"What are you saying? Are you afraid I'll blabber?"

"No not at all. But you can be made to talk, and we cannot. At present, the less you know, the safer you are."

Jesus, what do they mean by that? Will I be kidnapped next and given a truth serum?

"That has occurred to us," Jane responded.

The following morning, Aaron was informed that the US contingent was requesting another meeting with us. They had been refused entry when attempting to attend the first meeting, and apparently that had not pleased them. Security informed the director of the LHC complex that they threatened to withdraw US funding. It had been an ugly scene.

"All these events will play in our favor," Jane informed me.

I had no clue why they were important to my companions but decided to go with the flow.

It was clear that the US delegation had tremendous influence when the director of CERN requested a meeting with Aaron.

"The United States has used forceful tactics to press us to have you meet with them," the director told Aaron. He pleaded with Aaron to cave in and avoid a funding debacle as had been hinted at. The US contingent had alluded that visas for scientists visiting the United States could be withdrawn and US personnel working at the LHC facility could be instructed to return to their bases. It looked nasty.

After the meeting with the CERN director, Aaron returned and was as cheerful as ever.

"Things are going as well as I hoped," he said with a big smile. "Let's keep them worrying for a while, and then we'll reluctantly agree to meet with the US delegation. The news about us resisting the request will spread like wildfire through the scientific community, and that's great."

The meeting was arranged by the director of CERN, who acted as the intermediary. This time, there were six people in the US group. Joining the four delegates from the initial meeting was a representative from the US State Department, along with a scientist from the US National Science and Technology Council.

The six were all smiles, but that didn't last long. Colonel Jack Jones was again the leader of the group. They had guards posted outside the conference room, and Colonel Jones introduced the two additions, when we were seated.

He came right to the point. "After your previous refusal to share your findings with us, we briefed our president and the leaders of our scientific community. We have, in our country, devoted tremendous resources to the identical areas where you have obtained results, and I've been instructed to give you our utmost guarantee that this information will not be used for weapons proliferation."

"Then what does the United States want it for?"

"We want to utilize the results to generate clean energy," the colonel responded.

"How naive do you think we are?" asked Aaron. "Look at the track record you have after the first atomic test at Bikini Island during World War II. Now everybody has the bomb. You can practically order one on the Internet. No, I think we'll be safer if we keep this knowledge to ourselves for the moment. If, in the future, enough safeguards are in place, we'll furnish you with our decision."

The colonel looked flustered, but he was able to control his temper. "Would you be amenable to having us provide you with security during your stay? It will not be intrusive and will be only for your protection. We're concerned that harm may come to your group from terrorist organizations or fanatics."

Aaron was all smiles now. "Look, Colonel, you've tracked our whereabouts ever since our first meeting at Oxford, and we've felt very safe without your unsolicited efforts. We even know that you bugged our accommodations. Unfortunately for you, we were alerted immediately by our own detection devices and refrained from discussing anything sensitive. Please, go home and inform your authorities of our decision. This meeting has concluded for us. Have a pleasant trip."

When we were outside the building, I asked Jane about the bugging of our rooms.

"We knew, right from the start there would be attempts, but our sophisticated detection equipment had no problems locating them. Their primitive spying devices were just toys to us."

"Well, I'm glad we told them to get lost. I didn't believe a word they said about the assurances that they want the findings for peaceful purposes," I said.

"You and me both on that one," Jane replied.

"Well, if we're not going to do yodeling in the Alps, we might as well get the hell out of here. Does anyone have a different opinion?" I asked.

"No, I'll tell the director that we're leaving tomorrow. That's it," Aaron said.

The next morning, we were on our way to Afghanistan.

Kabul Polytechnic Institute

I was not looking forward to visiting another university, especially in Afghanistan. That country was in chaos with fighting factions, and heavily endowed with religious fanatics. Actually, the visit turned out to be pleasant, to my surprise. The hospitality of our hosts was outstanding. That, in itself however, was not sufficient to suppress my increasing restlessness, and I was getting argumentative with my companions.

"Why are we hanging out with another bunch of physical sciences geeks?"

"This is all part of our master plan. They'll make sure that our target country gets sufficiently interested in inviting us."

"If it is not too much to ask, which one is the target country of the week? I've not signed up to tour the world, and I don't want to be in the dark anymore."

"What do you mean?" said Jane. "I was hoping that we bonded enough for you to just enjoy my company."

What the hell is that supposed to mean? I thought, momentarily forgetting our mind connection.

"You know exactly what I mean. I know you love me and feel attracted to me," she said.

"You have to stop screwing with my emotions. That was not part of the deal. In addition, you're much too jealous for me. You would keep me on a short leash, and that's something I don't need." It was really upsetting, having her toy with me.

Then Aaron cut in. "You two can straighten your problems out after we have completed our job. Set your personal feelings aside and concentrate on the task at hand."

"Good idea. Now fill me in and tell me what the task is."

"Okay, here we go. Hold onto your hat."

"We've told you previously that the weapon technology and proliferation on your planet is of great concern to us, and we have been assigned to impede it. Our specific target is North Korea. That government has made nuclear technology available to Middle Eastern nations, and this rogue state is now in the process of developing hydrogen bombs. We've been tasked with disrupting their weapons development sufficiently to set them back at least twenty-five years."

"And the three of us are going to accomplish that? Good luck. I can imagine what kind of security they have at their facilities."

"Yes, but you're overlooking one thing. They're extremely neurotic and are always looking for better, more powerful weapons. You can be assured that they have keenly observed the spectacles we've caused over the last few months. I expect them to contact us very shortly, through an intermediary."

"Even if we're invited to their institutions, we'll have to be close to the weapon's development complexes. How do we accomplish that?"

"That won't be difficult. We're now in a position to hold our ground and insist on specific venues. North Korea has a number of high-powered military academic institutions, and one of these will approach us soon."

The next day, we were contacted by the Chinese embassy with an official invitation to military institutions in Beijing, China, and Pyongyang, North Korea.

"Our next stop will be Beijing University. China is the only superpower that has direct contact via embassies in North Korea, and they'll facilitate our visit. In the interim, I hope you like Chinese food. We'll be spending some time in Beijing. I expect it to be eventful."

"Talking about food," I said to Jane. "How will you fare when we have to dine with high-powered officials in Beijing and Pyongyang? I remember that you refused to have dinner with Eddie and me at my house on Long Island. These people will take it as an affront if you refuse to eat with them."

"Funny you should ask. I have been preparing myself to tolerate small portions of Far Eastern foods, and my digestive system is not complaining much anymore." She was all smiles.

Beijing

We were treated as celebrities, and the crowd at the Beijing airport was enormous; even common people were aware of us. TV stations, journalists, and some European newspapers were represented. Aaron was pleased.

"This sets the stage for our next stop. You can be sure that the Koreans are tuned into this spectacle."

It was pandemonium at the airport, and the crowd was swelling by the minute.

We had flown Air China, and the entire plane had been reserved by the Chinese embassy. At our departure from Kabul, the Chinese consul was present to wish us a pleasant trip, and a number of high-ranking military personnel were also included. Surely, our status had preceded us.

Since the flight had been reserved, the departure time was flexible. It had taken hours before we were finally seated. Drinks and hors d'oeuvres were waiting when we'd entered the cabin. What a spread. Jane had been next to me, and she'd stuck to me like glue throughout the flight. "Why are you so touchy?" I'd asked her at one point.

"I know what the Chinese flight attendants look like, and I have to keep you on the straight path."

"You're a jealous cat and very possessive."

"I can't help it. It's the fault of your genetic transfer to me. You can only blame yourself." I knew she'd be watching me like a hawk.

The service had been unbelievably great. Nonstop, throughout the flight, food and drinks had been constantly replenished. I had been on edge about the long trip, but this was a joy. The time had flown by.

After the welcome speeches at the Beijing airport and a brief address to the crowd by Aaron, we were shunted to waiting limousines, on our way to the hotel. The hotel staff was aware who we were and had been instructed not to treat us as celebrities. *So far, so good; I need a good night sleep*, I thought.

An entire floor was reserved for us, and security was posted at all entrances to prevent anyone from disturbing us. The bed was large enough for four people, and I quickly settled in. Before I fell asleep, I thought it would be nice to have Jane next to me to keep me warm, but I quickly dismissed the thought—too late.

"Just let me know when you're ready, and I'll be right there," she whispered on the telepathic link. She giggled; she wasn't serious.

I slept like a rock. This was the best place we'd been in so far. The breakfast variety was incredible. I had a hard time deciding what to eat and just stuffed myself. The old adage, "if it's free, load up," had occurred to me.

We did not have to pack. The place was reserved for our estimated two-week stay.

When we finished breakfast, we were informed that the officers of the PLA Military Academy had requested a meeting with us.

"It's scheduled for later in the afternoon," we were told.

Military guards were posted at every entrance to the hotel, and nobody was allowed into the building while we were leaving. When we walked outside, we were met by other hotel guests, gawking at us. Nobody had a clue who we were.

PLA National Defense University

I'd seen pictures of the plazas and streets in the city of Beijing with extremely large crowds, but today only a sporadic policeman was seen directing traffic on nearly empty streets. It was a strange situation.

"Chinese security is notoriously paranoid, and this is a perfect example," said Aaron. "The population has been ordered off the streets until we arrive at our destination."

At the university, we were immediately guided to an auditorium.

"It looks like we're meeting their military academics, rather than civilians as I had hoped," I transmitted to Jane.

"PLA stands for People's Liberation Army. What do you expect? We'd better be prepared for aggressive questioning about weapons development."

Our communications were now solely via telepathy, and in this environment, that was critical. I was sure that there were ears everywhere, registering every word from us.

"We can't afford any slips of the tongue," was Aaron's comment.

The provost of the university was a short, rotund general, who welcomed us with a broad smile. "So nice, you come to brief us on your breakthrough progress. We've invited the top specialists from our laboratories to participate in this important event."

The auditorium was nearly as large as the place we'd presented at in Oxford, but it was stark, with uncomfortable wooden seats on a bare floor. No luxury allowed in this place. All seats were filled with a mixture of uniformed and non uniformed attendees.

"A lot of state security here," was Jane's opinion. "We'll be squeezed for information, and they'll be relentless. Be careful with your replies."

Aaron briefed the audience on our progress to date and stressed that we were in the initial stages of our research. When he came to the part where he informed them that we would publish our findings in the established scientific literature, the provost stopped him.

"You mean we won't get preferential treatment?" He seemed genuinely astonished.

"When we're ready, we intend to make our findings known globally to the scientific community; everyone receives the same information."

The general was flustered and red in the face when he sat down. They had not expected this.

When Aaron finished with his presentation, the floor was opened for questioning. They came right to the point. A uniformed individual, covered with gold stars and stripes, stood up and introduced himself as General Zhang, the head of the physics and engineering departments. He addressed us as a group, but clearly figured Aaron to be the most senior. "We would like you to brief us on your state-of-the-art discoveries regarding dark matter energy."

Man, these guys aren't beating around the bush. That's pretty damn direct.

"Yes, and be prepared for more extremely aggressive questioning. Watch the juggling Aaron has to do in answering these questions in order to avoid revealing the status of our research," Jane replied.

"I'm glad they've overlooked me so far," I said to her.

She just had that confident smile, and nodded.

It was obvious that this gathering was only interested in weapon development, and their questioning was becoming increasingly hostile when Aaron replied in generalities.

"We've invited you on the premise that we would be informed of your latest status, and you're not providing us with concrete answers to our questions," said General Zhang. "We consider it an insult that you're not furnishing us with the material we're requesting."

"I believe my previous summation speaks for itself. We'll make our research findings available to all nations," Aaron said, while broadly smiling. "We've not indicated to anyone that we would reveal our discoveries exclusively to a specific party. We're concerned that they can be used for warfare improvements. Our research is purely oriented toward development of peaceful purposes. This planet is rapidly depleting resources, and you are struggling with choking air pollution in your cities. The nation with the most powerful weaponry will gain little if life on this planet becomes impossible to live on."

Maybe the audience realized that Aaron's response made sense because the silent concentration that followed was broken only by whispered discussions. Even the general sat down, seemingly absorbing the sudden change in direction this presentation was taking. It was as if they realized that having a powerful war fighting ability on a barren planet made little sense.

"I think this will be the shortest invitation in the history of this institution," I said to Jane.

"Yes, but it will make other weapon developers even more determined to access our discoveries. We must be constantly on the alert to safeguard our material."

Our hosts were pleasantly formal, but clearly unhappy when we departed. We went back to our luxurious hotel in the waiting limousine.

Cloned Again

"This meeting went as I expected," said Aaron. "Let's go to Jane's room, which I have checked for listening devices. It's clean."

"Why do you think they bugged our rooms and not Jane's?"

"They have a certain amount of prejudice against women, and they left her room unbugged for inexplicable reasons."

"I can't believe that General Zhang accepted your refusal for supplying our research data as our final position to his requests. What do you think their next move will be?"

"I think we'll find out very soon. Jane, and I used our monitoring devices to listen to their conversations, and they will do tonight what they have been ordered to do. Jane speaks fluent Mandarin, and we found their discussions very interesting. They're intent on getting their hands on our dark matter technology, no matter the cost. They have decided to interrogate you and get their hands on our data," said Aaron.

"Will they kidnap me?"

"Yes, but before you panic, let me explain our plan. That will take care of your worries. We'll make an exact copy of you again, but without your brainpower. We'll also make this clone impervious to pain by disabling his pain receptors. It will basically be a dead shell."

"Jane may get confused and start annoying the wrong individual," I joked.

"That's not funny." She was furious.

"You two, knock it off. This is too important," Aaron said.

"They'll have no clue why their interrogation methods don't work, and it will be fun to watch them get frustrated. We'll insert a tracking chip that enables us to locate their interrogation location. We'll hook into that facility with our monitoring device."

"And you know this will happen tonight?"

"Yes, they will send ninjas into your room tonight, so we have to get ready. You'll be hooked up to our devices again to make another copy of you, but it's just for the exterior. We have your DNA and RNA in our data bank, so your future is secure. We'll only transfer the absolute minimum DNA amount to your clone."

"What am I doing in the interim? I can't hide in the closet while they come to kidnap my other self."

"You'll be sharing Jane's room. It is the only one that gives us a secure location for you. Unfortunately, you'll have to stay in her room until we travel to our next destination. We're anticipating a follow-up invitation from a nonmilitary institution in this country because the authorities will not want to reveal the real intentions they had for inviting us. Are you ready for the copying process?"

"Yes, but I need an answer to the following. What are you planning to do with the clone after we leave the city? Kill him?"

"No, actually Jane had a good idea. When we're ready to leave, we'll call room service and temporarily drug the person who delivers the food. We'll copy his face and transfer it to your clone. We'll give him the ability to speak the local language and insert limited intelligence. You may decide on his IQ level."

"I think 130 should be sufficient."

"Great, he'll also have ample financial means when we sneak him out of the hotel. We'll supply him with the necessary papers to prove his identity, and he can deposit his fortune in a local bank."

"Does that satisfy you?"

"Yes, thanks."

"Are you ready now? We're somewhat pressed for time."

"Yes." I was now totally resigned to living with these two complicated individuals and their out-of-this-world methods.

We went to Jane's room, and the familiar process of making another copy was quickly accomplished. There was not a hair out of order. Exact, exact. I was still amazed by their techniques and the ease by which a task like making a clone was accomplished. In a half hour, I had been doubled.

"We'll leave your lookalike in your room for the time being and enjoy their body snatching spectacle tonight."

When all this had been explained to me, I looked at Jane's face to see if she had objected to having her room become my hideout for an unspecified period. I detected not a trace of discomfort. It looked like I was in for an interesting night.

Rude Awakening

Now that the clone was planted in my room, we thought it wise to order room service. "Better not take a chance, especially since the service is so outstanding here."

We had a great dinner delivered, while I temporarily hid in the closet.

I found it puzzling that their security had left Jane's room untouched with their listening devices.

Is it bad that they are prejudiced toward women? I momentarily forgot my connection with Jane. Her furious reaction caught me off guard. I had to profusely apologize to calm her.

When the room was cleared of the dinnerware, Jane produced the monitor.

"Let's see what's happening in your room."

I saw myself sitting on the bed, staring into space. The situation was unsettling, but the fact that he did not look unhappy calmed me. I realized that, at this moment, he was just a vehicle, produced to perform a task.

"When it gets dark, we'll see some action."

It happened suddenly. The lights in my room were shut off, and we heard a shuffle. Jane switched to thermal imaging, and we saw my clone being subdued and dragged out the room. Within a few minutes, the lights were back on and there was no trace of the events. It was disturbing and fascinating to me.

"You two can keep an eye on the interrogation developments. I don't expect them to do anything tonight. They'll need instructions from the PLA on how to proceed. I'll be in my room if you need me."

Aaron left, and I wondered what would happen next.

"We have one bed, rather large for both of us to share," Jane said.

She's definitely not bashful— I caught myself, but it was too late.

"I'm well aware how you feel about me, and you don't have to be nervous. I just want to experience the thoughts you have about me. I don't need sleep and just want to feel your physical contact. I think you call it spooning."

She looked at me expectantly, but I had no answer. This situation was both pleasant and unsettling. It would be our first interaction in, what I fully expected to be, a sexually charged atmosphere, but I was in for a jarring disappointment.

"How do you normally sleep? I regulate my body temperature at will and can easily adjust to new situations. I think you should touch me, and let me feel what your contact does to my emotional being," she said.

She was nearly undressed—just wearing panties and a bra. She had an incredible body, and my testosterone began to act up.

"I can't understand why you're willing to experiment with lovemaking. I'm not even sure that you have all the necessary equipment, since you cannot bear children."

"Don't worry about that. I'm fully functional, and I want you to desire me. I have been prepared by our physiologists, but that's only theory. I want to experience it."

"Do you want the lights on or off?"

"I want to see what you're doing to me, so lights on please, "she said.

She took off her panties and her bra. Lying next to her naked body really turned on my desires. I decided to check out her reflexes and toughed her in the erogenous areas where I'd had much success in my previous life. No reaction.

"What are you doing?" she said.

"I'm checking whether your wiring is intact."

"What does that mean? Is that another derogatory expression from you?"

I was still thoroughly aroused and expected her to be turned on, but nothing happened.

My attempt to join with her produced only questions. It wasn't working. She was a lifeless entity. The result was predictable. I quickly fizzled and that was it. I was supremely disappointed.

She acted puzzled and ready to analyze why I was behaving strangely. "Didn't you like it?" She asked.

"Not really. In my previous life, I had better experiences."

"Why do you say that? I did cooperate."

"In this department, you'll have a lot to learn. You may have the brains, but emotions are lacking. Let's go to sleep. This was work for me, and I'm tired."

"You're strange."

"Yes, but you aren't much better."

"Can we please spoon? I want to feel that."

"Okay, for a short time. I need my rest."

The next morning, she told me that the night's spectacle had confused her.

"I think lovemaking is overrated," was her position.

"I agree with you," was my assessment.

"I was trying so hard to please you, and you don't appreciate my effort," she said.

"The process was troublesome for me, and you can feel free to blame it on my unstable personality. Let's forget the whole episode. We'll concentrate on our assignment from now on. Sharing the bed with you was not my idea, and it affected me having you near me, but it didn't work out. On a cosmic scale, it was a ripple," I said.

"Agreed. I just wanted to experience the feeling. Now that I know, I'm satisfied," she responded.

The Interrogation

Aaron entered Jane's room, and we were ready to track the interrogation procedures on the monitor. "It may disturb you," Aaron warned me. "But remember he cannot feel any pain, no matter what they do to him."

I expected to see my clone's torturers using their favorite method of shoving bamboo under the fingernails, but they started by shining bright lights into his face. The lights, directly in the clone's eyes didn't affect his pupils—no contraction. The interrogators were surprised that it didn't cause the expected reaction and ordered more powerful lights. It still produced no reaction from the clone.

Jane was translating and we were amused by the interrogators' consternation. Even their verbal threats had no effect. "Get the doctor," Jane translated. "I think this guy died from the ninjas' manhandling."

"Well, he's breathing."

"I don't care. Something is wrong. Get the doctor."

After a while, the doctor showed up and checked the clone's vitals. "Nothing wrong with him physically but I don't like his reactions. It almost seems that he's detached from reality."

"Smart guy, that doctor," said Aaron. "We've done a good job, and they'll get nowhere with their questioning. Soon they will sneak him back into the hotel."

"I want to do one more thing. Give him truth serum."

The doctor produced a hypodermic needle and gave him an injection.

"Is that scopolamine, like in James Bond movies?"

I guess it was a dumb question because they both had a hearty laugh.

"That's an outdated drug; it will be somewhat more powerful," Jane said.

To the interrogators' consternation, the drug had no effect either. It was fun to watch.

After one more day of constant questioning, they decided to return him. That night, a number of shadows entered the room again, and my other body was back.

The next day, we tapped into the PLA quarters of General Zhang. He was outraged that no information was obtained. "What kind of shit interrogators did this job?" he screamed at the team leader of the abduction unit. "I should have done this myself."

We observed the spectacle from the safety of Jane's room and were pleased with the outcome.

"Tonight we'll finish turning your copy into a Chinese individual by giving him brain power and the use of the local language. He'll have his freedom and certainly deserves it."

It was carried out without a hitch, and I slept alone in my room again. I was actually pleased that Jane was not my bed partner. In my wildest dreams, I could not have imagined that I would be happy to be without her.

We were waiting for another university invitation and wondered when the government would decide what to do with us. The PLA provost had a number of high-level meetings, and various scenarios were discussed. We were tapping into their conversations from the safety of Jane's room. Some were outright ridiculous and ranged from arresting us to deporting us to Vietnam. Cooler heads prevailed, and it was decided to issue an official invitation for us to brief the faculty at the University of Science and Technology, at Hefei, the capital of Anhui province in Central China.

We were told we would be flown to Anhui the next morning. Our departure from Beijing was cloaked in secrecy. The drive to the airport was in a limousine with tinted windows, and the airplane was parked in an empty area of the complex. There was one stewardess and two cockpit personnel. That was it. We were snuck out of Beijing like thieves in the night. The trip was fast—only 550 miles, and we landed two hours later.

There was a small welcoming committee but no press or television. I didn't mind. I was looking forward to a quiet day for a change.

The North Korean Delegation

I t was not clear why the PLA allowed us to make another stopover in their country. Maybe they were hoping we would inadvertently slip up in a less hostile environment.

"This is one of the foremost technical institutions in the country, and they have an excellent research department. They even have a synchrotron radiation facility. We can look forward to some interesting questioning," said Jane.

The trip to the hotel was short, and we only had the driver and the representative of the university to accompany us. No security detail.

"Maybe they learned their lesson, not to pressure us."

"Unlikely. They're pretty relentless, and I expect their military to show up again," Jane said.

The hotel was not as luxurious as the place in Beijing had been, but I didn't mind. I just wanted to get a good night sleep without any distractions. Jane's presence, next to me, came to mind. We had separate rooms, and I retired early. Slept like a log.

Next day, we were scheduled for a meeting with the faculty, and after a nice breakfast, we were on our way.

The meeting was held in a large conference room, instead of an amphitheater. We were welcomed by the president of the institution, and after a short speech, he excused himself. We were left with the physics and engineering staff. I had not expected this and wondered if it was another ploy to get us to cooperate with their request for more details of our research.

We had an interesting meeting in the morning and I was pleasantly surprised that no military personnel were present. That, unfortunately, lasted only until lunch. Instead of lunching in the cafeteria with the staff, we were shunted to a large dining room in a separate building.

"This is where we usually have lunch with important visitors," we were told.

An additional ten individuals had joined us for lunch. Four of them were introduced as North Koreans.

"What the hell are they doing here?" I asked Jane via our silent link.

"I'm not sure, but it's serving Aaron's purpose."

Discussions during lunch were cordial and relaxed. No threats from anyone. I began to wonder what would happen when we resumed our morning discussions. I didn't have to wait long.

When we returned to the meeting room, the six previously unexplained individuals were introduced as Chinese observers, whose assignment was supposedly to assure our briefing would not be hostile. We were told that they were not military, but I found that hard to believe. Their mannerisms and responses to orders from their commander easily gave them away. I was bracing for another unpleasant meeting.

The Koreans were acting differently than the Chinese, and it became clear that their purpose for attending was only to prepare us for an invitation to their country. It was not clear what their hierarchy was within their group, until one was introduced as the consul of the diplomatic corps in the province of Anhui. *He's a big wheel,* I concluded. The Koreans were extremely polite and did not participate in the technical discussions. They only observed.

The Chinese academics were well versed in dark matter and black hole status of the current scientific literature, and their questions were probing but polite. It was different from our last encounter with the PLA crowd. We were informed that this day would be devoted to discussions, and the next day we would be shown their synchrotron facility.

The tour of the synchrotron installation was interesting for me, but apparently it was boring for Jane. "This is a toy for children in our world. Your scientific community has a long way to go before it can produce anything of substance here."

"Well, how about the LHC in Switzerland? That's a formidable enterprise, and they're discovering many new particles," I said.

"Yes, that was a nice accomplishment, but your scientists are still only scratching the surface."

"Well, I can't argue about these things. I'm not up to speed in these matters, so I'll just agree with you. That's the easiest."

"Don't be passive. I like having a good argument with you, but you'll need to know the facts," she said.

After the tour, we went back to the conference room, and results of our latest findings were presented. Aaron was treated again as the senior scientist of our threesome, and I could relax and listen. Occasionally, Jane would give me her opinions on our silent link, and I could process some of the events in my mind, while being disconnected from the meeting.

"Stop daydreaming," she said. I knew she was bored herself.

The meeting finally came to an end, and we could retreat to our rooms for an hour. After that, we made a mandatory appearance in the dining room, where our hosts served an elaborate dinner. I felt like a pregnant snake when I got back to my room. I assumed I was done for the night, but Aaron had a different idea.

"We'll outline our plan about approaching the North Korean scientific community and how we'll whet their appetites," he announced. "We'll have to make sure that their military is sufficiently intrigued to invite us to their complexes."

"Good luck," I said. "They are neurotic to the limit and will not respond favorably."

"We'll feed them just enough information about dark matter to get them interested," Aaron replied.

Coral Castle

"You guys have been giving me all these vague facts about dark matter but have never explained, or shown me proof, that you've mastered the intricacies of using it. Why don't you give me something concrete so I can understand what's so special about controlling those forces."

"Okay," Jane responded. "We're planning to do this anyway, and now is a good time. What we'll reveal will sound unbelievable, but it's absolutely true. Have you ever heard of Coral Castle in Florida?"

I had a vague recollection of the eccentric accomplishments that were performed by one person, all alone in the dark of night.

"Well, let me give you an idea why what he did was unusual. He alone moved blocks of coral that a crane would have difficulty lifting over large distances on his property. How do you think this was possible?"

"I have no explanation for it, and I can't wait to hear from you how it was done."

"Simple," she said. "He was one of us."

I had braced myself for another unbelievable explanation but had not expected this.

"You must be kidding. Was he actually one of your transplants?"

"That sounds nasty," said Jane.

"I'm sorry, but you two give me plenty of reasons to question you. The alien explanations are becoming more difficult to believe. Insulting you is the last thing on my mind, but I need proof that you're not snowing me."

"Okay, fair enough. Here it comes," said Aaron. "His name was Edward Leedskalnin and he lived from 1887 to 1951. He was my best friend and was sent as an observer to earth, not to intervene or intermingle with the earth population. When he was twenty years old, measured in your years, he met a girl and fell badly for her. Unfortunately, she was not interested in marriage, and her rebuff hit him terribly hard. He retreated into obscurity and lived quietly for a few years in Florida."

"This is all great, but what does it have to do with moving the blocks around all by himself?"

"I'm coming to that. Give me a chance. I was sent to earth to convince him to return to our dimension, but he steadfastly refused."

"I'm going to build a monument in honor of my love, and then I want to die on earth. I don't want to return to my birthplace and exist without her," he told me.

"As you can see, he lived sixty-four years on earth and died. He could have lived forever in our dimension had he so decided, but he died of a broken heart instead."

"Are you telling me that both of you can live forever, by choice?"

"Yes. We weren't planning to divulge those details to you, but you're forcing us to do so. We want to be totally honest with you and answer any question you have, with one exception. If it does not jeopardize the mission, we'll completely level with you."

"Does that apply to both of you?"

"Yes, both of us," they said simultaneously.

Good, then I can ask Jane some intimate questions, I thought before realizing that she registered every one of my thoughts; too late. "Be careful what you ask me," was her message.

"Back to the matter at hand," Aaron said.

"We'll now explain how Edward moved these unliftable, twenty-seven-ton blocks alone at night. He used the power of dark matter that we have harnessed. This, we're also planning to use during our infiltration methods into the North Korean weapons complexes."

"Wait a minute. I would like a better explanation about the manipulation of heavy objects with the use of dark matter forces. You yourself have refused to supply details because of the inherent danger of supplying this knowledge to earth scientist. How did this Coral City builder get away with using those forces?"

"Because we cannot make people return against their wishes, and we ourselves are not allowed to intervene in earth matters. We've already told you; that's the reason you've been recruited to assist us."

"So you're telling me Edward went rogue?"

"Yes, that's the case. I was sent many times to try to convince him to return to our dimension, but he was adamant. Building his monument, and dying on earth, was his decision and I could not stop him," Aaron said.

"Okay, what dark matter force did he use to manipulate those weights? You've issued warnings about the danger of the strong side of the force, so I assume it must have been the weak one?"

"That's correct. We can manipulate the weak force and use it to our advantage to penetrate the North Korean nuclear installations and storage areas."

"So, how did this compatriot of yours move those blocks?"

"He counteracted gravity by reversing the weak force polarity. Gravity is normally assisted by the weak force when the two operate in tandem. When he reversed it, he effectively made those blocks weightless."

I now started to realize why Aaron and his people wanted to keep this technology away from the military. The capability he was describing would have enormous ramifications, and would be disastrous in the wrong hands. "Okay, I believe you," I said. "My question now is how do we apply this operation to the nuclear arsenal of the North Koreans?"

"Well, one thing at a time. I hope we have convinced you sufficiently to not question our honesty anymore. We've but one objective and have been instructed to carry it out at all cost."

"Oh great, all cost? Does that mean sacrificing me if necessary?"

"We will risk our own existence if required. We must be successful, and eventually you'll realize the criticality of our endeavors."

"One more question. Was Jane in on the selection of me for this operation?

"Let me answer that," Jane said. "Yes. I became intrigued by your survival instincts during the war and how you enabled your family to survive those five years of German occupation. For an underfed child of between seven and nine years old, you did remarkable things." *Well, at least I know she was involved from the beginning.*

"And how were you selected for this?"

"I volunteered to be a member of our group because I have researched extensively the control and manipulation of dark matter. I'm a science adviser to our counsel, and some members objected to me taking on this critical task, but Aaron prevailed. He selected me for this important undertaking."

"Was that the only reason?"

"No, it was not, but I'm not prepared to tell you the personal aspects of my decision."

So, she has a secret that I'm not supposed to know about.

Then the instant response—"Yes, in due time you'll find out."

"I don't think it's fair that you can hide your feelings from me while I'm an open book to you. I seem to hit a barrier when I attempt to read your feelings for me and have to rely on you conveying them to me. Do you think that provides for a level playing field?"

She looked puzzled and did not seem to understand why this bothered me.

"Look, I don't block you from accessing my emotions, but you have not reciprocated that access into your mind. I want to know why," I persisted.

"Why don't you tell him the real reason right now," said Aaron. Jane replied, but her answer did not register with me. They could still leave me out of their conversations if they wanted to. "This is just the perfect example that proves my point," I told her. "You exclude me without giving me the reason."

"I've been prohibited by the authorities in my dimension from allowing you to have unbridled access to my mind. I know that is disturbing to you, but I cannot do anything about it. For now, it has to stay that way. I'm sorry."

I decided to drop the subject for now and return to reality. "What's going to be the approach to get the North Koreans to invite us to their secret installations?" I asked.

"That's going to be tricky without revealing too much to them," Aaron noted. "We're contemplating giving a small demonstration in a secure laboratory for the North Koreans only. We don't want the Chinese scientists to be present for this demo. The North Koreans are so secretive that they'll not reveal to anyone what we're going to show them. I'll request a side meeting with them while Jane keeps the Chinese happy. She'll discuss their current collider design and point out that their power output, even though it's projected to be multiple times more powerful than the LHC, is insufficient."

"Will you need me for your demo?" I asked Aaron.

"Yes, you're the interface. You'll control the operation with the monitor."

"How do you suggest we accomplish that?" I wanted to know. "They'll see it."

"No, I'll insist that you must be shielded via a screen. The reason will be the need for concentration on your part."

The Real Reason

Jane's explanation for not completely sharing her thoughts with me had been on my mind constantly, and it caused me to be sullen and depressed. I could not hide anything from Jane, and she let it ride for a day before cornering me. "I know full well what the reason is for your state of mind, but I can't do anything to eliminate your obsession."

Calling my condition an obsession really hit a tender spot. "You have to be kidding me to call it that. You're digging around in my mind at will, and I have no clue what you're really thinking at any time. Unfair isn't even the right word to describe it, and I'll tell you this! You either have a viable explanation for not allowing me to share your thoughts, or I'm out of our agreement."

Jane looked stunned after my emotional outburst and started crying. I had expected her to lash into me and call me unreasonable, and her reaction greatly disturbed me. "Come here and let me hold you," I told her.

She sobbed on my shoulder for a few minutes and then composed herself. "I have felt your frustration since my explanation for not allowing you into my mind, but I need special permission to disable that blocking. It has been imposed by our security personnel, and I cannot remove it."

"You can tell those bureaucrats that I'm out of the game until the reason is explained to my satisfaction, and it better not be a matter of trustworthiness. They should by now have discovered that I keep my word."

At that moment, Aaron appeared, and Jane and he had their private telepathic discussion, annoying me even more.

"You guys really don't get it, do you? I'm totally fed up with this situation, and I don't want to see either one of you until it's resolved. I went to my room and closed the door. *To hell with them and their crappy reasons for excluding me from their private thoughts and discussions*, was my thinking. *If they're not getting the message, they're out of luck.*

· · · · · ● ● ● ● ● ● ● ● ● ● ● ● · · ·

The next morning, Aaron and Jane were waiting for me when I got out of the bedroom.

"Are you ready to listen to the official decision that has been reached by our officials?" Aaron asked.

"Yes. I hope it's believable," I warned.

"Jane is more equipped to explain the intricacies of the security barrier that exists between us and other species," Aaron said.

"Well, sweetheart, let me have it," I said to her.

"If the barrier between our minds is removed, it will give you complete access to not only my scientific knowledge but also to the total picture of our world's defenses. That cannot be allowed under any circumstances, even if it results in you canceling your participation."

Now it started to make sense to me. It had nothing to do with Jane or Aaron. Their national security would be at risk if I were privy to all their secrets.

"I understand the objections by your government, but is there any way the barrier can be partially modified to allow me access to Jane's emotions? Right now it is somewhat lopsided to have her roaming around in my head and depriving me of the same ability," I said to Aaron.

"I've explained the dilemma to our scientist, and they promised me that they would use all their resources to arrive at a solution. Does this satisfy you for now?" she said.

"Yes, honey, this makes sense to me, but I still would like to have some of the barrier removed."

"Give this time, and maybe a solution can be found. Are you ready to concentrate on the task at hand?"

"Yes, I am."

"Good, let's discuss the next phase."

The Chinese Collider

Remarkably, the Chinese were not concerned that we split into two groups. I suspected they wanted design concepts of their collider kept from outside eyes, even though it was advertised as an international undertaking.

"They're hoping for breakthrough information from us," Jane told me afterward.

She gave them an impressive technical briefing on our theoretical discoveries that had discovered the minimum capacity to produce a small black hole and the requirements to contain the resulting dark matter. She covered magnet shapes, minimum ring circumference, and different target materials. She stressed repeatedly that we had not remotely produced a substance that resembled dark matter in a laboratory, but that did not discourage their questioning. In particular, power requirements and the theoretical limit to produce dark matter were of tremendous interest to them.

"I had difficulty telling them what the real issues are in producing a small black hole in a primitive collider," she told me afterward.

"What do you mean with primitive? Their machine will be many times more powerful than the Swiss LHC."

"True, but it's still insufficient to produce even a tiny black hole. It took us many eons to get results, and they're not capable of reaching the power levels necessary to reach anything viable."

"How are you planning to give them that depressing news?"

"I will spread that out over the next few meetings I have planned with them. When the time is ripe, I will present them with the parameters and design of an installation that will be so prohibitively expensive that even collective efforts between nations can't afford it."

· · · · · · ● · · · · · · · · · ·

During the next few weeks, Jane spent most of her time with the Chinese design crew. Primarily, these discussions centered on the theoretical parameters, and she purposely delayed giving them the depressing information. Finally, she decided it was time to spring the bad news. I outlined our design concepts for a futuristic collider that had a six hundred-mile circumference, with ten thousand closely shaped magnets in a dual ring. This is what our research indicates. It's the required minimum to produce a black hole.

"When I gave them the design requirements, they were stunned. They had no questions for a while and just sat there, digesting the information. Their senior scientist finally spoke up and thanked me for my informative presentation."

"It may have been informative, but I'm sure they were not pleased with the material you provided," I said.

"Well, afterward, the scientists had an animated, loud argument among themselves. They did not realize that I was privy to everything they said since I'm well versed in scientific, technical Chinese. Their opinions ranged from being convinced I'd lied to wanting to get their hands on our research results, by any means. They were clearly not happy with the information I had supplied."

"So you gave them one of your snow jobs?"

"Yes, but it is not in my nature to lie. I was uneasy doing it."

"Why? I don't think you have been honest with me with all your answers."

"I told you; that's not my fault. From the start of our interaction with you, I have been constrained by my government's security policies. Our dimension is very security conscious, and having my mind fused with yours was considered a risk by our agencies. Only Aaron's influence made it happen. And let me ask you this; how do you think it felt for me to have to hold back on giving you the details you're entitled to?"

"I believe it was hard on you. Fortunately, no damage has been done to our relationship, so let's drop it. I would love to peek into your mind, but if it can't be done, I'll live with it."

"I have been instructed to wait to be completely open with you until the barrier issue is resolved, and that's okay with me too," she said.

Aaron's Demonstration

It was necessary to make an indelible impression on the Koreans, and Aaron had a special plan. "You and I are going to give them a demonstration of our capabilities by elevating a heavy object in front of their eyes."

"Where is this to take place? And how will I be involved?"

"You'll be in the room with me, behind a screen, out of the Koreans' eyesight, and you'll manipulate the dark matter weak force via the monitor."

We left in the morning. Aaron carried the invisible monitor to the auditorium. The Koreans were already assembled and looked at us expectantly. "We'll blow their minds with our demonstration," Aaron relayed. And we did.

Aaron gave them a short introduction about the power of the weak force and then told me to get ready.

"My colleague needs optimum concentration and cannot be distracted, which requires him to assist me from behind this screen. Aaron gestured for me to get ready. I found an empty table behind the screen. "Just feel where it is. When you touch it, it will become visible."

When I felt it, it instantly appeared and lit up. "I'm ready," I told him.

"Good, you'll have contact with Jane's technicians, and they'll manipulate the object. Just follow their directions. Don't forget—all communication between us via telepathy."

Aaron's image appeared on the monitor, showing a desk in front of him with a large steel ball in the center. "I'm going to elevate this, but you'll have to focus the beam on the ball and move it vertically until I tell you to stop. I'm also in contact with Jane's people, and your job is to keep the beam's position on the center of the ball. This is a coordinated effort between us," Aaron said.

The technician instructed me to how to position the beam and wait for Aaron to initiate the lifting.

"Okay, I'm ready. Go slowly by moving your finger up the screen."

When I moved my finger a fraction of an inch, the ball began lifting about an inch off the desk's surface.

"Keep on going slowly, until it's about ten feet in the air," Aaron directed. He stood like a magician with his hands in the air, pointing at the floating ball.

I heard excited talking from the room, and I knew the audience was impressed.

"Now, lower it slowly."

When the ball rested back on the desk's surface, the Koreans were ecstatic. Thundering applause echoed through the room.

"Come out of your hiding place and take a bow."

I thought he was kidding, but he insisted. High-ranking officers were standing on the podium next to Aaron, and they applauded me when I appeared from behind the screen. They shook my hand and kept telling us how impressed they were. The presentation had been a success.

Aaron told me to leave the monitor for him to take back. "Go to your room and rest. You deserve it."

Aaron did not return for the remainder of the afternoon. When he returned to his room, he called us over. "Do you think we were you successful?" I asked.

"Well, elevating the heavy ball in the air astonished them," Aaron replied. "They didn't expect it."

"How did you accomplish that feat? Are there more capabilities this monitor has that I should know about?"

"Yes, when this device is connected to our computer systems, it has tremendous powers. In time, it will be explained to you. For now, it is better to leave it at that."

"Can you at least give me some idea how you accomplished it?"

"Okay," he agreed. "I had access to our quantum computer banks via the monitor you manipulated. Monitor access was linked into our labs, and the computers reversed polarity of a small amount of dark matter to have the weak force negate the gravity subjected on the steel ball. They obviously thought I was a magician levitating somebody."

"What was their reaction to this demo?"

"After you left, they almost guaranteed me an invitation to their university and access to their labs. They will brief their 'Dear Leader', and that will be sufficient to get an official invitation."

"So my empty monitor can do more than look into my past?" I asked, remembering the time Aaron had roped me into joining them.

"You have no idea about the power of your five-dollar 'empty' box," Aaron said, smiling. "We'll have to demonstrate much more of the device's capabilities to the next group in Pyongyang," he added. "I'm sure they'll be mostly military."

"I thought it was illegal to interfere physically into our world's affairs. Doesn't this qualify?" I asked.

"Partly it does, but this is an extremely critical situation. I have obtained special dispensation from our council to execute this mission, and this demonstration to the military brass will be essential. I intend to levitate a sixty-ton tank before their eyes."

"Well, if that doesn't blow them away, nothing will."

The next day, the Koreans returned home, and we spent another week having small meetings with the Chinese faculty. This had become routine for me and did not affect my sleep anymore. What did bother me, however, was when Jane alluded to a purely personal reason for being on this world tour with me. It happened after we resolved the security and mind-reading issue I had pushed for. I tried fishing a few times, but she was steadfast.

"When the time is ripe, I'll tell you," she insisted. "It will just disturb you."

She was an expert in keeping me hanging.

The Pyongyang Invitation

As expected, the invitation to Pyongyang University arrived at the end of the week. It was hand delivered by the North Korean consul and included a personal note from their 'Dear Leader', who was looking forward to our beneficial visit. I wondered how we would handle their excessive expectations.

We decided to take the trip to Pyongyang by train. Jane's opinion had been that the Korean airline companies did not have a good maintenance record for their aircrafts, and I had not been looking forward to flying either. The distance was about seven hundred miles, and the train trip would take ten hours.

At the Korean border, we were met by heavily armed border guards. They were polite, but suspicious, until Aaron showed their captain the invitation from their 'Dear Leader'. After that, they did not stop bowing. A number of phone calls were made, and within an hour, a local Korean welcoming committee arrived. They were embarrassed and told us that the Chinese had not informed them of our decision to go by train. Jane had activated her Korean language capabilities and was amused by the angry discussions she overheard. "Those sons of bitches did it again," they were saying. "Every time we invite a scientific team to our installations, they pull this shit. They're worried about our progress."

Jane was informing us about the events, and I found it interesting and amusing.

"This is a little more than professional antagonism. The Chinese are worried about the nuclear progress the Koreans are making, and they also want it curtailed."

Meanwhile, the train had been in the station for a long time, and angry rumblings from the other passengers were becoming noticeable. The captain barked orders, and the passengers were ordered off the train. He issued a warning, and not a word was heard from the people standing in the cold with their luggage. The whole train was emptied.

"Security precaution," said Jane, who had overheard the proceedings. "This is what happens when you live in a country where you have no freedom or rights. These people are stranded until the next train arrives, probably later in the week. Welcome to the 'Dear Leader's' paradise."

Meanwhile, the consul with his delegation arrived and profusely apologized for the accommodations.

"We've ordered a dining car, and you'll continue your trip in comfort," was the explanation for the delay. I was actually enjoying the spectacle of all these people bending over backward to please us. It was clear that they all feared punishment if we had a single hair out of order.

A number of train cars were uncoupled, and the remaining cars were occupied by still more security personnel. An additional locomotive was added as a safety precaution, in case one had a breakdown. Their rail system had a reputation for having a poor maintenance record as well, and we weren't surprised.

At least we're not six miles up in the air. I would need a few strong drinks flying their hardware, I concluded.

All stops were eliminated, and we arrived at the central rail station in Pyongyang in record time.

"This is where the hard work begins," was Jane's message.

The Korean People's Army's Ground Force (KPAGF) is the main segment of the North Korean defense forces, and Aaron expected it to be the largest component of the welcoming party. He was right. Predominant among them were uniforms with impressive ranks, including a field marshal and many generals. I found it worrisome.

What the hell are they expecting?

"You worry too much," said Jane. "We have it under control."

"I followed the situation in North Korea from a safe distance in my previous life, and I know they don't treat saboteurs nicely. I'm glad that I'm just a tool in this dangerous mission. If anything goes wrong, you and Aaron go back to your world, and I'll continue living my drab existence in the United States. It's a win-win situation."

Jane looked very serious and, after a long time, replied, "I guarantee that no harm will come to you during this mission. I'm capable of protecting you, and you should believe that."

"You have no idea how relieved I suddenly am," I replied sarcastically.

"Okay, drop it. You two are at it again. I'll also make sure that no harm comes to you, so assume this mission will have a positive, exciting conclusion for you," said Aaron. That was it. The message was simple; go to bed and sleep it off.

The Mole

T he next morning, we had a grandiose breakfast. I was rapidly getting used to being spoiled with exotic food and knew this could not last forever. If we got through this ordeal without being executed for espionage, I'd declare myself a winner.

When we got back to the large conference room, only military personnel were present. I was sitting comfortably, not listening to the droning by the Marshal about the importance of our discoveries to the security of their nation, when I picked up a telepathic message from the audience. How was that possible? No earth person, besides me, could possibly have that ability. I looked at Jane, and she seemed as confused as I was. Could the Koreans have planted somebody to trip us? How was that even possible?

Whoever was doing this obviously saw our consternation and transmitted an assurance. "I'm one of you and am here to assist you in successfully completing your assignment. We'll talk later, in private."

Even Aaron now seemed taken aback.

The meeting lasted until mid afternoon, and all military personnel left, except one general. We were on edge, not knowing what to expect from this strange telepathy development.

"My name is Cheong. I'm the head of internal security, and the assumption is that I'll attempt to convince you to cooperate with our military and share your discoveries with us. My real purpose however is to assist you in accomplishing your assigned task to dismember the nuclear arsenal that we have accumulated." All of this was communicated telepathically.

I thought I was the only one who was floored by this development, but my two companions looked just as confused.

"Are you one of us?" Aaron finally asked.

"Yes, I'm the offspring of a male from our dimension and an earth mother. My father taught me to communicate via telepathy. I'm sorry to have startled you, but I had no choice."

This was an incredible development—an insider with the rank of general in charge of their security. What a fortuitous event.

"I hope you'll understand that I'll have to discuss this totally unexpected development with my two colleagues. I also will have to brief the council, and cannot make a decision of this importance without their approval. Can you travel to our dimension, if required?" Aaron said.

"No, I'm sorry. I've never acquired that ability. It was not passed on to me."

"We'll have to digest this monumental occurrence and plan accordingly. I'll brief the council tonight, and I'll inform you tomorrow of their decision."

Unveiling

A military escort was waiting outside the room, and the general instructed the soldiers to accompany us to the waiting limousine.

"Tomorrow we'll have a private meeting in my quarters," he transmitted. He saluted and left us standing, shocked about what had transpired.

When we got back to the hotel, Aaron asked us how we'd interpreted this unbelievable luck that seemed to have befallen us.

"Well, if this guy is for real, then our chances have improved exponentially," was my opinion. "He can provide the access to their secret research areas."

"I agree, but we better make sure that he's for real. He could be lying about this whole deal," said Jane.

"He can't be lying about one thing though. To my knowledge, it was impossible to acquire telepathic abilities without having at least one parent from our dimension, prior to the first ever change we made to your genome," said Aaron.

"Could the Koreans have made this breakthrough without your assistance?" I wondered.

"I can't believe that. We'll have to assume he's genuine," said Jane.

"How about him being from a dimension other than your own?" I wondered.

"That has occurred to me, but it's highly unlikely. We have the ability to detect any being from another dimension in our vicinity. It causes a ripple in our aura, and we'd have instantly noticed the presence of an outsider. I'd rule that out."

"Then maybe we're just extremely lucky to have him as our partner. I have been wondering how we could possibly penetrate their security barriers, and this may be our only chance," I said.

"You're right," said Jane. "Other than using force, it would have been impossible without his assistance."

"So you two agree that we have acquired a collaborator, and I should recommend to the council that we make him the fourth team member?" asked Aaron.

"Yes," Jane and I said simultaneously.

"I agree to have him as our partner but how will we safeguard our discussions, knowing his ability to listen in on our telepathic transmissions. Can you block his access?" I said.

"He has only the basic skill to communicate. There are three levels—basic, intermediate, and advanced. You have the middle one activated, and Jane and I can operate on any level, being advanced."

"Ah, I have noticed in the past that you two could exclude me, and I thought it was a trust issue. I assume it is for security purposes, yes?"

"Absolutely. We have total faith in you, and you have to believe that. Unfortunately, we both have to live with the directions that the council has dictated, and sometimes we must exclude you. Eventually, that will all change. I'll now have to brief them about this unexpected development and obtain approval to proceed differently than we'd planned. I'll leave you two to entertain each other."

Aaron disappeared, and Jane and I were left alone in my room.

"Would you like to be alone," she said with a smile.

"Not necessarily, but I want you to refrain from playing games with me. I still cannot figure out what your purpose for sleeping with me was, and it's disturbing. I like you near, but not that close, if you don't mind."

"Not a problem with me. I'm still learning how to deal with your species, and have also some issues with the adjustment."

"You know, your choice of words isn't exactly impeccable. We generally associate species with zoo animals. I hope that's not your intention."

"Not at all, just a poor word choice. I'm sorry if I offended you."

That's a crock. She knows full well what she meant.

"I was truthful. You must believe me, since I cannot easily lie."

The following morning, they were both waiting for me in my den. At least they gave me the privacy of staying out of the bedroom. I was anxious to hear what the council had agreed to and did not want to wait until after breakfast. "Tell me how we should proceed," I said in greeting.

"Well, this whole chain of events was entirely unexpected by me, and I assumed the council would also be shocked. And they were. They did not know about the plant in the North Korean defense forces. Only one official in our world received valuable intelligence from him. Placing him in the intelligence apparatus in preparation to assist us had required careful orchestration."

Even Jane seemed surprised. "Why was I not informed?"

"This was deemed to be so critical that only two individuals had knowledge—the mole whom we just encountered and our director of interplanetary security. For years, he has operated in total isolation, and nobody in our dimension was aware of his existence."

"I was under the impression that your dimension had no contact with other worlds."

"That's only partially true. When cosmic security is involved, we're allowed to cooperate."

It seemed that this development had been preplanned and would hopefully facilitate our dangerous incursions into the extremely well-protected bomb storage areas. My unease diminished a hair.

Planning

After breakfast we were escorted to the quarters of our newly acquired accomplice, the general. He had a luxurious three-room suite in a building that was designated as the internal security facility, shown in large, gold lettering over the entrance, Jane translated. This place was sprawling, and the entrance hall looked like the best hotel we had stayed in. The recently found addition to our team was the head of this organization. Not bad. I was impressed.

The security detail consisted this time of eight solders—four in front and four behind.

"Talk about neurotic—as if we can stroll through this building unnoticed," I noted.

"The more security they have, the better. That'll reduce their suspicion about our intentions, when we're closely watched. It all fits into our plans. Stop worrying," said Jane.

The general's suite was filled with brass. Even the marshal decided to make an appearance.

They have high expectations about us, for sure, I thought. Before I was even finished with my thought, the general looked at me and indicated that he expected me to be quiet. "Go with the flow and do not comment," was his transmission. This guy was used to giving orders.

It surprised me that these high-ranking members of the Korean brass weren't pushy. They were certainly more diplomatic than their

Chinese counterparts had been with their direct approaches. After an hour of cordial conversations, the general ordered everyone to leave.

"We'll have a secure discussion and I want to interact in private with our visitors."

"How can he get away with that?" I asked Aaron.

"I think he's cleared for the highest security level and can exclude everyone. That, in conjunction with telepathy, will make our interactions a lot easier."

"Agreed, but we still have to be very cautious. There are many undefined variables in this equation," Jane said.

"Wow, that's sophisticated language. I'm impressed," I joked.

"Sarcasm will get you nowhere," was her retort.

I'd actually started enjoying needling her and getting her riled up.

When the room emptied, I expected the general to outline his plans, and I was surprised that he resorted to telepathy.

"This whole facility is bugged, and we can only discuss generalities using our voices. Any discussions pertaining to our logistics have to be done via telepathy. Be careful. We can't afford to slip. I'll be vulnerable if we arouse suspicion."

"I'm General Cheong, head of the security division of our glorious defense forces. I have been instructed to make your visit beneficial for my nation and to assist you in any way during your visit. You've been cleared to enter most of our research facilities but certain restrictions apply. Some of our defense complexes will not be accessible to you, and I'm sure you understand our reluctance to reveal our most advanced capabilities. Most of the world is treating our peaceful endeavors as hostile intentions. Our 'Dear Leader' decided, in his infinite wisdom, to protect our nation against enemies and develop a formidable defense capability. We feel safe in the knowledge that we have an adequate deterrent." This part of his speech was intended for home consumption and done via voice.

"You can be sure that it's all being recorded," transmitted Jane.

Aaron responded by assuring the general that we would be

accommodating to the utmost in providing our latest research parameters—all via voice.

His assurance pleased the general noticeably, and he assured us again verbally that our visit would be beneficial to his nation and to us.

This was obviously the propaganda phase—to placate the listeners. I wondered what would be next.

We talked some more generalities, and then General Cheong got serious.

"Only telepathy, don't forget. You'll have to give an impressive demonstration to the general staff that will convince them that it's essential for our defense forces to obtain the ability to control the forces that are the constituents of dark matter. We've obtained all the material that you have presented during your previous university visits, and our leaders are intent on obtaining your results at all cost. It will be a delicate balance for you to feed us sufficient details about your progress but not enough to enable us to manufacture any destructive capabilities. Even in our private discussions, I'll talk to you as if I'm the antagonist. I have to make certain that I don't slip up myself. Don't draw any conclusions from that. I'm fully dedicated to destroying our nuclear stockpile and capabilities."

Talk about double agents—I felt like I was part of a movie plot.

The Weak Force Potential

We had a sumptuous lunch, and I had interesting discussions with people who joined us. I almost forgot why we were here and the seriousness of the situation. Even my compatriots were enjoying the luncheon. We continued with the formalities after lunch. General Cheong invited the group back into his quarters, and Aaron agreed to have an informal question and answer session before the general presentation, which was scheduled for the next day. The group respected the limitations that Aaron had delineated, and their questioning was surprisingly civil. It was almost like psychological warfare to me. There was nothing to antagonize us. I wondered if this was all part of a well-structured plan to have us cooperate. The meeting continued until mid afternoon, and then General Cheong announced that we'd have to go back to our hotel to prepare for the next day's formal demonstration.

We had our escort back to the hotel and were alone to plan for the important event.

"You'll have to control the demonstration process, and it will be the same as the ball levitation, except it's more extensive. It again will be powered via the monitor interface with Jane's technicians," said Aaron.

Parts of my short fuse were still operational, and they were annoying again. "I finally understand why I was recruited for this operation. Even though I realize I'm a minor entity in this operation, it still annoys me that you gave me all those fancy reasons for my selection. You could've used any earthling for this operation if it's only for operating the monitor. I'm starting to realize that I'm just the fifth wheel in this operation—the necessary item in this operation that provides the physical interface between our worlds. That seems to be all my role amounts to."

"You don't have to be dramatic. Without you, we cannot accomplish our assignment, and we've always known that your participation is essential. You're wrong to assume otherwise. Now relax and listen to our plans," Jane said.

"We'll connect into our quantum computer banks tomorrow, and you'll elevate a sixty-ton tank. This is a major undertaking, and it will make or break our purpose of impressing the ranks of the defense forces. My technical staff will be connected telepathically to you and will instruct you about the intricacies of performing this operation. It has never been done and only our analysis has assured us that it's feasible to perform this operation. Don't get flustered and drop the tank," Jane said, smiling.

"Can I have a dry run?" I asked.

"No, I'm sorry. It's a one-shot deal." *Well, there goes my restful night sleep.*

"You can do it," Jane whispered." I have utmost confidence in you."

The Monitor's Power

In the morning, my anxiety level had peaked to a maximum. This whole enterprise now depended on my ability to interface with computer banks in another dimension. *How the hell did I ever let myself get talked into this?*

The weather was balmy, and the plaza was filled with at least a thousand spectators, predominantly uniformed. In the middle of the plaza was the star of the show. It was an enormous tank, its turret ominously pointing in my direction. A temporary podium had again been constructed for us, and my area was screened off from view. Aaron insisted that this was necessary for me to concentrate on the delicate procedure I would be performing and had convinced the Koreans to construct this barrier. General Cheong was privy to the reason I had to be shielded from the audience.

After an introductory speech by our team member to the troops in Korean and a very enthusiastic, very long period of applause, we were ready to start.

I touched the monitor and immediately connected telepathically with Jane's computer technicians. "We've never attempted this before and have calculated a 50 percent probability of success," they informed me.

I guessed that was the techs' way of bolstering my confidence that it would be successful—nice going.

The display showed the plaza and the tank placed in the middle.

"What you have to do is position your index finger on the tank to calibrate our systems."

As I touched the monitor, I noticed a slight tingling and wondered what it meant.

"It means that you're connected to our computer banks," was the answer.

"Oh, I guess I'm hooked in, yes?"

"Yes, let us know when you're ready."

"Well, now or never. Let's do it."

"We'll start slowly, at half power. You'll be instructed on how to focus all power on the central gravity point (CG) of the tank, or it will topple."

I noticed a slight vibration in the monitor and heard a loud uproar from the crowd. For a split second, the monitor displayed a simultaneous view of the plaza and the tank. I had been concentrating on looking at the tank's CG point and did not notice that the tank had lifted a few inches off the ground.

"Give me more power," I told the operators.

"It's unpredictable what will happen," the team leader said.

"I don't care. We have to convince them of our ability to control the weak force."

"We'll link three more processors; that will give you eight. Our projection is that it will lift the tank 50 feet in the air."

Sure enough, the tank slowly rose higher—to the jubilation of the crowd. Then it stopped elevating, just hanging there.

"Now comes the difficult part. We'll disconnect one processor at a time and gradually lower this large weight. We can't rush this."

The technicians on the other side of the connection did a great job. The procedure worked flawlessly. "If this doesn't blow them away, nothing will," transmitted Jane.

When the tank was resting back on the plaza surface, the crowd went wild. It took a long time before they calmed down. General Cheong gave them a pep talk about the importance of this demonstration and what this technology meant to the country.

"When we acquire this capability, nobody will threaten us anymore," he said.

Minor detail, I thought. *It will take a while before they have the computer power to control this process.*

"That's why we're not concerned about giving this impressive demonstration. Your nations don't even have working quantum computer prototypes. We're not worried about the dangers of earth nations accessing dark matter forces. It can't be accomplished for many millennia," said Jane.

"How can you be so sure?"

"I'm the foremost quantum computer expert in my world and have worked with these machines most of my life. Is that convincing enough?"

"Will do," I said.

"So this demonstration was solely organized to provide access to their facilities?"

"Yes, and that's important enough."

After many handshakes with high-ranking uniformed brass from the audience, we were allowed to go back to the hotel.

When we got back to our room, Jane said, "Can I give you a congratulatory kiss?"

"Why do you want to do that?"

"I've been studying your earth customs, and that seems appropriate after such a successful afternoon."

"I'll allow you to kiss me on the cheek, but that's it."

"What else is there?" She looked surprised.

"I'm not willing to divulge that information to you because kissing will have disturbing consequences for me. Please forget it."

"Do you mean you won't let me kiss you to celebrate?"

"I prefer if you don't. It's not good for my psyche. And before you disappear, I have a question."

"Okay, I'll answer it if I can."

"I actually have two questions. I have been wondering how Aaron's friend accomplished the lifting of the blocks at Coral City. Did he have access to your computers?"

"Yes. This was a period in our world where security was not expecting illegal accessing of our computer systems. It has since been corrected."

"How can you be sure this won't happen again?"

"Our computers at the time of the illegal accessing did not have the safeguards we have added since then."

"Can you be a little more specific?"

"Our early Quantum processors were only designed for high volume data manipulation but had no independent decision making logic. After the Coral City incident I was tasked with my scientists to add a neural processer front end. This is a symbiotic design where the neural unit compares the operator's genome parameters to the stored genome data. Only if the internally stored genome is identical to the DNA and RNA of the technician, access is allowed. This technique is foolproof."

"And secondly, how could I communicate with your techs if my telepathy range is only fifty feet?"

"That's one of the powers of the monitor. Distance is irrelevant when it's used for transmissions."

With that, she disappeared, first saying over her shoulder, "I'll see you at dinner."

I didn't believe she was disappointed about my kissing refusal.

......●........

Everybody was in a festive mood during dinner, and it was clear that our circus performance had produced the results we'd hoped for. I expected it would facilitate our access to North Korea's highly classified development labs. Dinner stretched into the early evening, and the strain of the day was taking its toll.

"You look tired," General Cheong said. "You have to get some sleep."

Aaron overheard the suggestion and told me to excuse myself.

"We're not tired, he transmitted. You should sleep well after your outstanding performance of today."

I slept solidly for ten hours.

The next morning, we met at breakfast, and I was informed that the day would be devoted to small group meetings with the North Korean scientists.

"I would like to excuse you from these meetings, but you've become a celebrity here, and they will want to congratulate you and ask questions. Be vague and do the best you can. Jane will back you up," said Aaron.

Again I was greeted by a festive atmosphere as I entered the dining room. I was definitely a hit. Being in the presence of these high-powered military people and scientist, with the knowledge that we would inflict irreversible damage on their accomplishments gave me a strange feeling. I momentarily felt guilty and wanted to leave the room, but Jane intervened.

"Suppress your emotions and realize what would happen to your world if this country obtained our knowledge. They willingly starve their population to fund the military, and they have the largest standing army in the world. They have to be stopped, and you're the key to our success. I'm incredibly impressed with your performance, and I'll soon tell you how I would like to reward you."

"What? Am I getting the booby prize?"

"Please, don't make fun of me. I'm serious. You're still not conditioned enough to accept my proposal, but I'm confident that you'll be pleased."

Jesus, she has another riddle for me.

"Blasphemy is not necessary," she said angrily.

The Next Phase

General Cheong arranged meetings all week with resident scientist, and I was bored. The same questions and answers were becoming annoying, and I was restless. "I thought we were visiting Pyongyang University? We have been inundated with the military all week. Can we not request some time at the university?"

"What's the difference? Everybody we meet here has the same goal. Obtain our secrets to facilitate bomb production. Don't be naive. The university is crammed with military personnel too. It's all the same. Their collective desire is obtaining our knowledge."

Giving it some thought, I came to the conclusion that Jane was right. I should not deviate from the purpose of destroying their weapons of mass destruction.

After two weeks of excellent food at all meals but lackadaisical attendance at the meetings on my part, the big decision was made by the general. We were to inspect North Korea's underground facilities, where their nuclear devices were researched, manufactured, and stored. That was our initial target.

The next morning, after breakfast, we were met by a small military convoy that would transport us to the underground site. We were alone in a modified, locally built Humvee that had sufficient seating for the three of us, plus the driver. The driver had been personally assigned by General Cheong, who had also arranged for us to travel without a massive escort.

I'd actually expected to be blindfolded during this trip. Obviously, the general's rank was not sufficient to make this unilateral decision. He must have convinced his superiors that it would be important to treat us with kid's gloves and not irritate us.

We played innocent and asked what our destination would be. They politely refused to answer. It did not matter since General Cheong had informed us telepathically where we were headed. We would be visiting the Geumchang-RI underground nuclear facility, about three hundred miles south of Pyongyang. The trip would take approximately seven hours. Jane informed me that this facility had been inspected twice by the United Nations, and the inspections had not revealed any suspicious nuclear-related activities. After the last inspection, the complex had been converted to accommodate full bomb production; bombs were in storage at this facility.

"This is where things get serious," said Aaron.

We were welcomed by the commander of the base, accompanied by a small group of civilians. "These are the scientists who work full-time at this facility." They were all smiles.

"Don't let their demeanor fool you. Many of them are here against their will, while the government holds their families hostage. They have little choice," said Jane.

We were escorted to a large hall, where, to my surprise, General Cheong was waiting for us with the formal welcoming committee. We listened to the usual speeches about the importance to the nation of receiving our research findings. After handshakes and a brief speech, we were shown our accommodations—clean, roomy, and stark. No luxury allowed on a military base.

I was tired from sitting in the bouncing truck and announced that I would like to rest for a while.

"I'm tired too," declared Jane, "and will rest a while also."

I must have looked surprised because she transmitted that she wanted to be alone with me. *Now what? Does she have another proposal to shake me up?*

"Yes, but you can always refuse," came the answer.

We had adjacent rooms, and she gave me an hour to lie on the bed and gather my thoughts. I wondered what she had in mind this time. She was not known for beating around the bush and came right to the point. "I have given this considerable thought and have concluded that I want to be your life partner."

"What? Are you crazy? First of all, I don't know what that means, and secondly, I may not even come out of here alive. You can't be serious."

"Yes, I'm serious. I have acquired a strong affinity for you that I cannot explain myself and have concluded that we belong together."

"Well, this is certainly an unexpected development, and I need time to think this over without having you in my head reading all my decisions and emotions. Can you please turn off your damn ability to read my mind? I really want to be alone to digest this matter."

"Sure, take all the time you need."

So far, other than our failed attempt to join, Jane and I had had a platonic relationship, and I could not fathom how this would change if I agreed to her bonding proposal. I would certainly stall on making any decision until this task was completed.

And what does a life partner mean with a female from another dimension? Remember—she found lovemaking overrated. If you agree to her proposal, you're nuts.

Evolving Events

A fter the jolt that Jane delivered, I was actually able to take a short nap.

I must be getting used to this crazy existence.

A polite knock on the door woke me up. Four soldiers were at the door, smiling and bowing. "Your presence is requested in the welcoming hall."

My two companions were already seated, and I wondered what would be next. The commander of the base was also a general, and he apologized for the stark facility we would occupy for our duration. "We're not known for luxury," he joked. He quickly got serious.

"I have viewed the video of your impressive demonstration, elevating the tank. My superiors have obtained permission from our 'Dear Leader', and we have been instructed to give you full admittance to our development laboratories and manufacturing areas. Outside of our weapons assembly complex, you'll have complete access. In return for this privilege, we would like to be fully informed of your latest research status, and we'll give utmost priority to being able to duplicate your tank elevation ourselves."

"Sure, nothing to it," transmitted Jane.

"It is going to be difficult to hold this determined group off indefinitely; we must move fast," I transmitted. "How do we accomplish that?"

"I'll explain, after we have toured the laboratories and are back in our room. It's all under control," was Jane's relaxed answer.

The lab tour was interesting for me. Their equipment was up to date and clearly obtained from other countries. I saw markings in French and Russian and wondered how the companies that supplied these items had circumvented the embargos that were in place.

"There are always back doors available; money talks."

"Yeah, I agree. Corruption is everywhere. That's bothered me for a long time."

"Maybe we can do something about it in the future," Jane whispered.

The tour lasted most of the afternoon, and we were released.

"Dinner at six," we were informed.

When we got back to our rooms, Aaron wanted to meet immediately.

"I need an hour for showering and getting my head around today's events," I said.

"Fine, we'll give you a short break. Don't make it a habit," Jane said, smiling.

I needed time to digest these whirlwind developments. First Jane's proposal had shaken me up pretty good, and then the insistence of the base commander that we supply the North Korean military with the information that would enable them to make objects weightless. I started to doubt that we could possibly have success with our mission.

When my allotted time was up, Jane and Aaron knocked on my door.

"All conversations nonverbal, at all times," Aaron reminded me.

I came right to the point. "What concerns me most is how we're going to hold them off without making them suspicious. They will watch every move we make."

"I know, and here's my plan" said Jane. "We know that utilizing the weak force requires enormous computer power, which is not available on the base. The first requirement I'll state is that all the other bases they have for nuclear development be linked together. This is not a trivial operation and will take them at least a month to accomplish.

Even then, we know that it will be insufficient to even suspend a gram of material. It will stall them long enough to carry out our next phase."

"And what is that, if I may ask?"

My two companions looked at each other, and Jane nodded.

Apparently, this was a biggie. I braced myself for another impossible task.

"I assume you remember some of your physics lectures from your distant past, because this involves the atomic structures of their bomb cores. As you know, the core consists of uranium 235, and we're assuming that with their relatively low yield devices, this core contains about five pounds of fissionable material. We have to neutralize the bomb cores without them realizing that they're not capable of delivering a nuclear explosion. Does that sound impossible to you?"

"Ever since I linked up with you, I've erased that word from my vocabulary."

Jane and Aaron thought my answer was funny, but I was dead serious. No matter how crazy their ideas were, they always had a solid foundation.

"Okay then, let me explain how we plan to accomplish this. Do you remember the periodic table from your college courses?" I had a vague recollection of the topic, but it was buried deep in my mind.

"Let me refresh your memory. If you look at uranium on the periodic table, you'll notice that its atomic number is 92. It has seven energy levels, where these levels are occupied by their respective 92 protons.

Directly below uranium, on the periodic table is protactinium, which has atomic weight of 91. This also has seven energy levels, and the only difference is the fifth energy level in uranium, which has one extra proton. The six other energy levels are populated identically between uranium and protactinium. With our focused weak energy beam, we can reduce the number of protons in the uranium from 92 to 91 and change the bomb core. This operation requires the dislodging of one proton from each uranium atom, changing it, thereby, into protactinium. This will take an incredible amount of narrowly focused weak energy, which will be controlled by the supercomputer banks in our dimension."

"Sounds a little more complicated than toying with a tank. And how many computers will it require? The bombs are certainly well protected in their storage areas by a half mile of earth and formidable concrete and steel shielding."

"We realize that, but you have no idea what we're capable of. I have instructed my technicians that a quarter of our dimension's computers will be on standby, dedicated to this task. If you realize that a single quantum processor has the computing power of all earth's computers combined, our ultimate success will seem feasible," said Jane.

Uranium atom number of protons:
First energy level: 2
Second energy level: 8
Third energy level: 18
Fourth energy level: 32
Fifth energy level: 21, versus protactinium's 20
Sixth energy level: 9
Seventh energy level: 2

Protactinium atom number of protons:
First energy level: 2
Second energy level: 8
Third energy level: 18
Fourth energy level: 32
Fifth energy level: 20, versus uranium's 21
Sixth energy level: 9
Seventh energy level: 2

Orientation

H aving free reign on the complex grounds gave us the opportunity to explore every building without triggering suspicion. Aaron decided that we should individually investigate the research laboratories and engage the scientist in discussions. We should explain our ultimate goal of utilizing the power of the weak force and emphasize its potential.

"You may exaggerate, but don't go overboard," he warned.

The scientists were eager to explain what their specialties were, and we acquired valuable information about the status and details of their nuclear developments. We did this for a full week and became intimately familiar with the layout of the complexes.

In the interim, Jane had informed the base commander about the necessity of linking the computers at the surrounding bases with his base systems. They had not expected this and were not pleased to get this information. "That's nearly impossible," the commander told her. "These systems are all dedicated to their base operations and have no exterior connections."

"We require enormous computer capacity, and this is absolutely essential," Jane insisted. "Without it, we cannot focus the weak force energy."

They were shocked to hear this and were scratching their heads for sure.

Then they asked the question I had expected, and worried about.

"How were you able to suspend the tank without having access to our computer systems?"

"For that, we hacked into the European Astronomical Society computer network that monitors the night sky for unusual events. Many thousands of these computers are linked, and we were able to 'borrow' a few minutes of their combined, integrated processing power."

"Did they buy that explanation?"

"Yes. It sounded far-fetched, but they had little choice. They saw the demo, and it made them believers. The old expression, 'the bigger the lie, the easier it's accepted,' worked in this case."

We saw General Cheong intermittently, and I was wondering if he was planning to interface with us at all. Even though we were now well acquainted with the layout of the labs, we still didn't know where the battle-ready bombs were stored or how we could pinpoint their storage locations.

The Underground Test

A nother week passed, and we were coasting. Meetings with the scientists were now routine for us, and I got to know some of them personally. Some confided in me that they had been recruited from the university and forced to work on the military bases. Their families were held hostage by the government, they said. I was getting the feeling they would be willing to help us derail the advancement of bomb production. When I mentioned this to Aaron, he was all over me.

"Don't fall into that trap. Half these scientist are members of the intelligence community, and they are here to prevent internal sabotage. That keeps the fear factor high. If they talked about being dissatisfied, it's a setup, for sure."

Wow, innocent me; I'd almost bought the subterfuge.

· · · · · ● · · · · · · ·

Finally, General Cheong informed us that we would be allowed to witness the planned underground nuclear test and should be equipped to spend two weeks in a remote area of the country. The location was unknown to us.

"If we're to succeed in derailing this test, we will need the approximate latitude and longitude of the location," I said to Aaron.

"I know, and we're working on that," he answered.

I found his response annoying and vague. "Well, I actually have some interest in the success of this mission, since my life may depend on it. If you don't mind, I would like some details."

The two resorted to communicating on the level that was out of range for me, which made me furious."

"Are you two idiots still worried about me spilling the beans?" I yelled on my connection to them.

"No," was the calm answer from Jane, "but we're worried about their interrogation methods. They're not pretty, and you would not survive them. Are you willing to take that chance?"

"Yes, I am, and I want details now."

"Okay, General Cheong will plant a tracking chip in the immediate vicinity of the device they are testing, and we can zero in on the precise location. Then, when you operate the monitor, we can focus the beam on the core and make it inert. They'll have no clue why it failed to explode."

The Remote Test Range

The following week, we took another trip in our Hummer. But this time we weren't alone. General Cheong and some one hundred personnel were in the convoy. Apparently, there was no adequate airstrip to land his private jet near this remote testing range.

"He might as well suffer like us," I joked.

"It's a good thing you're not using your voice. They interpret these jokes as insults."

What a godforsaken, crap country this is. How do these people get through the day?

"You can get use to anything, if you're born into it."

"Yeah, getting used to things is becoming the order of the day, being with you two."

"Are you being sarcastic?"

"Me? I wouldn't think of it."

"It's time for you two to lay off with the banter," Aaron inserted. "We have to do some serious planning and integrate this with our dimension. It will be delicate and complicated to say the least. Do me a favor and keep your personal differences to yourself until we've completed our mission."

We arrived at our destination in the late afternoon. It was barren, mountainous terrain, with a sparse number of buildings. "I'm sorry, but we all have to live in barracks for two weeks. We'll make up for it when we get back," General Cheong joked.

Well, at least he has a sense of humor.

"When this is over, you'll have to teach me some of your humor categories. I'm having difficulty understanding why that was funny," Jane said.

"Don't feel bad," I told her. "There are many humorless people walking the earth."

We had been on the base for about a week when we got shocking news. The North Koreans had accomplished what the United Nations deemed impossible. They were testing a miniature uranium bomb with triple the explosive power than had been estimated to be feasible by the eight other nuclear nations on earth. This was stunning, and it cemented even more firmly that it was imperative that we successfully complete our mission.

Each evening, while supposedly sleeping in the barracks, my two companions would disappear for the night and return in the morning. Aaron was busy coordinating his affairs with the council, and Jane was supervising the linking of the computer networks.

All I could think of now was the essential success of our mission. If the North Koreans were able to make this device small enough to be launched on one of their missiles, the whole Asian continent would be threatened. There was no doubt in my mind that South Korea, North Korea's neighbor on the other side of the demilitarized zone, would be their first target. The North Korean government had, for years, threatened Seoul with annihilation, but that was with conventional warfare. A miniature nuke could wipe out the city, along with its ten million inhabitants.

Aaron had outlined our plans to the council and obtained carte blanche approval to make our intervention a success by any means necessary. They also offered to enable general Cheong's intermediate telepathy level, but Aaron had refused. "It's not a matter of trust, more of safety," he had told them.

"If we can sabotage their test with our planned approach, we'll be able to get approval for any resource necessary in my dimension," Jane said. "All we have to do is be successful."

Aaron had apparently broached the subject of protecting General Cheong after this affair was completed. I had some private worries about the punishment—possibly execution—he would receive when we suddenly disappeared, and it worried me. Jane knew this, as I had casually mentioned my concerns.

"It will be taken care of," she'd assured me. "We don't abandon anyone who assists us in our efforts."

I waited anxiously for the message from General Cheong that he had successfully planted the tracking chip. It took all week before we got a brief telepathic message when we saw him in the cafeteria.

"All set," he transmitted. That night, Jane made her last departure to assure her power supplies were functional for the next morning's operation. This was the make or break event for us. The countdown was to take place at dawn. We were in the barracks, and I viewed the events on the monitor. The nuclear device was mounted on a pedestal in a cave. Countdowns had always been nerve-racking to me because they were frequently stopped ten seconds before a missile launch in the United States, where I had seen launches from Cape Canaveral on TV. For this test, they started the count at three hours. It was agonizing.

I had the monitor in front of me and checked numerous times the exact focusing of the beam on the core location, inside the nuclear device. The bomb was small. I estimated it to be around three feet in diameter—small enough to put in the trunk of a car. Now, with so many fanatics in the world, they could drive this into the middle of Seoul, and North Korea could claim innocence. This had to be stopped.

Finally, the countdown reached ten seconds. I activated the beam and felt the slight vibration in the monitor screen. Nothing visibly happened, but also no detonation occurred when the count reached zero.

"We were successful," Jane said, planting a kiss on my cheek. "You did a very nice job."

In importance, the kiss ranked second. I was beside myself that we had pulled this off. The aftereffects of this failure would reverberate for a long time through this tactical nuclear base.

· · · · · · · · ●● ● ● ● ● · · · · · · ·

We did not see general Cheong for two days, after the failure. He said that finger-pointing had been the main outcome after the failure because nobody had been able to offer a justifiable explanation. The shaped charge in the device had detonated and destroyed the core. It was partially radioactive from the non-fissionable jacket that surrounds the nuclear uranium core, but less so than had been expected from the fissionable uranium. Tremendous pressure was put on the scientific staff to analyze the failure, and a number of possible explanations were offered to placate the generals. None of the analyses of the bomb fragments pointed to the real cause of the failure to trigger the nuclear explosion. Their scientific team had to conclude that an unknown malfunction within the device had caused the mishap. "It will be a serious setback in their development of a miniature device," said Aaron. "Phase one is complete."

We were now confident that our method could be used to neutralize the North Korean's existing stockpile, provided we were able to access their storage facilities. Something had puzzled me about the ability of our weak force beam to remove protons and electrons from the uranium core, and I posed the question to Jane. "That was the difficult part of this procedure," she explained. "We had to bundle two separate focused beams of antiprotons and positrons to neutralize the released protons and electrons from the uranium core. We had to annihilate these particles to avoid handing the scientist a clue."

"What do you mean, a clue?"

"Presence of those particles in the cave would have been a scientific enigma, and we had to avoid that." *Not much of an explanation, but good enough for me. As long as the evidence is taken care of, I'll be happy.* "I thought it would be adequate. I can't make you too smart yet," she said.

Tremendous pressure was put on the scientists to explain the cause of the failure. In their desperation, they requested that we be part of the investigation team. We thought it was ironic, and I enjoyed the moment. I felt sorry for the people who were under the gun but was pleased that they were getting nowhere. We explained that bomb construction was outside our area of expertise, but they insisted we should be part of the investigative team. "We'll have to resort to a wag."

"What does that mean?" asked Jane. "I have never heard that term."

"This comes from my experience during proposal times at the aerospace company, where I was employed in my previous life."

"Fine, but what is the meaning?"

"Well we used it when we were forced to give estimates about unknown complexities of a job we were bidding on. It stands for wild ass guess."

"Not funny. Keep this stuff to yourself." At the meetings we attended, a number of causes were offered, but it was clear that the scientists had not been able to detect a trace of our interference with the test. They directed a number of questions at us, but Jane was able to deflect them nicely. "This is outside our area of expertise, and we can only provide an educated guess," she replied. "How about a wag?" I transmitted.

"You're crude," was her terse reply.

Locating the Stockpile

We attended two more meetings but it was evident that we had nothing to contribute. The Korean scientists recognized that weaponry was not our area, and they struggled on their own. Some high-powered officials from Pyongyang had been visiting, but not even this pressure produced results. They were at the stops and couldn't find the reason the test had failed. So far, so good, we concluded.

Now our next task was to neutralize the rest of the stockpile. We planned to use the same method, but had to locate the storage facilities first. We had sporadic short meetings with General Cheong, but he was always surrounded by members of his security team. We needed to meet him in private, and he transmitted to us that he was having difficulty arranging that. "If we are careful and use telepathy he should be able to meet us in the presence of his troops, "I said.

"If we inadvertently slip-up he'll be a dead man. And so will you for that matter," said Aaron. "We can't take the chance."

Finally, when the Pyongyang brass had left, he was able to set up a meeting in his room.

"Telepathy only," he reminded us. This is becoming dicey."

Aaron pointed out that it was essential that we know the location of the storage places and the number of devices we had to neutralize.

"I understand. And I'm planning a trip with my security team to inspect the storage facilities."

"Do you know how many we have to disarm?"

"No, that information is highly classified. But I have been able to discover that fifteen were fabricated to date. I don't know if they're all operational, but we should assume that's the case," said General Cheong. "They have to be stored in separate areas, and you'll have to provide me with fifteen tracking chips. They have to be unobtrusive. When I inspect each complex, I'll hide them as close as possible to the bomb locations."

"Will it be a problem if we can't pinpoint their exact positions?" I asked.

"Yes and no. We can handle a certain amount of uncertainty by compensating for the radiated power you control. Not being familiar with the layout will introduce this uncertainty, but that can't be helped," said Jane.

"I can make only one inspection trip to avoid suspicion, and I cannot stall them very long. Everybody is strung out from the pressure, and they're eager to find the cause of the failure."

"Blaming sabotage would get them off the hook, so let's not give them a reason to arrest me," said Cheong. *Point well taken*, I thought.

"Yes, he's right. This will be exceedingly difficult," Jane said.

That night, Jane and Aaron disappeared into their dimension and did not return for three days. When they returned, they showed me fifteen microscopic chips, each barely distinguishable from a grain of sand. I marveled at their technology.

General Cheong's Security Inspection

H e was gone for two weeks and returned with mixed results. "Their storage areas were practically impenetrable," he told us. "And we were never allowed into them without being escorted with personnel from base security. We were closely watched. I inspected twelve storage complexes and was able to leave the tracking devices in each room. I was unable to obtain any details about the possible two additional bombs that my own investigation had presumed to exist. We should assume those are stored in a different area."

Well, that was both good and bad news. We would have to disable all devices, or North Korea would still be able to explode one over a city. It was well known that this regime would stop at nothing and would severely retaliate if they suspected sabotage by the Western Nations. I fully expected they would use a functioning device and explode it over South Korea. The general also presented details about the shielding that was part of the complex. "I took a freight elevator down and timed how long it took to reach the storage area. It was five minutes. At an estimated descend rate of five feet per second, the facility would be fifteen hundred feet under the surface. Could your device penetrate that much earth and an unknown amount of concrete?" he asked.

"Yes, we could reach the center of the earth, but power is not the issue. The logistics involved in disabling each device, without having exact parameters of the size and construction of these bombs, pose special problems. Are the devices uranium fueled, or possibly fueled by plutonium? We must know that. If we're dealing with plutonium, the process will be more complicated, and I cannot guarantee success," said Jane.

"Can we use the same method of changing plutonium to its neighbor's on the periodic table?" I wanted to know. I asked this question on the private telepathic level General Cheong didn't have access to.

"Why are you keeping Cheong out of the loop?" said Jane.

"I think, the less he knows, the safer he is," I responded.

Jane seemed surprised by my answer, and said."He's heavily involved and we shouldn't keep anything from him. We can't keep him in the dark about our methods. We'll use the low telepathic level so he knows how we're proceeding." She told me on the intermediate level and then switched to the lower level.

"The atomic structure of americium is again similar to plutonium, with only one energy level being different. This is the next atomic number in the periodic table above plutonium. However, we would have to insert an additional proton and electron into each atom, which is more complicated."

Plutonium atom number of protons:
First energy level: 2
Second energy level: 8
Third energy level: 18
Fourth energy level: 32
Fifth energy level: 24, versus americium's 25
Sixth energy level: 9
Seventh energy level: 2

Americium atom number of protons:
First energy level: 2
Second energy level: 8

Third energy level: 18
Fourth energy level: 32
Fifth energy level: 25, versus plutonium's 24
Sixth energy level: 9
Seventh energy level: 2

"The fifth energy level of americium has one more proton than the plutonium level, 25 versus 24, and requires the insertion of an extra proton in this level to change plutonium to americium. This will be difficult to accomplish. We must find a method to analyze whether we were successful in changing these two elements. I'll discuss with our scientists whether we can analyze the reflection of our beam. To my knowledge, this has never been done and this ability will be critically important to our success. We'll have to know what constitutes the cores of these bombs."

Jane left and Aaron decided to confer with the council. I hung out with myself. It had been a hectic week, and I deserved some rest.

My companions stayed away for two days. I was nervous about arousing suspicion and being questioned about their absence, but nobody was concerned about us at the moment. Base personnel had their hands full defending their conclusions about the failure and realized from our last meeting that we couldn't provide them with assistance. Jane returned first and appeared to be concerned about the ability to determine the core composition of the bombs. "We could not simulate the conditions of the storage areas and had to make assumptions," was Jane's gloomy assessment. "The reflected signal was weak and contained large amounts of interference, which obscured the parameters. It will be very challenging, and the results will be uncertain. My team has put its maximum resources on this problem, and I hope they can improve on the present results."

"What are our chances?" I asked.

"If my team makes progress scrubbing the reflected signal, it's about 50 percent, otherwise, it will be much lower. When Aaron returns tonight, we should attempt to inspect one of the storage areas and analyze the size and design of the bomb. Maybe we can determine some salient facts. I suggest you get some rest. It will be a long, stressful night."

········•••••●•••••••····

Aaron and Jane woke me for dinner, and afterward, we retreated to our quarters. Jane suggested that we attempt to inspect an area in order to gauge our power requirements for penetrating the depth. She had arranged to have twenty-five processors linked, and we randomly selected a location where the tracker device was placed. We got an immediate strong signal return and a clear picture on the monitor. We scanned the surface of the bomb for markings and noted a number, printed on the side—94.

"Unless I'm too optimistic, this is the plutonium atomic number. Let's check the next one. This was also 94, and the next four were also numbered identically. I started to believe that it was a peculiar numbering system for their inventory. However, luck was on our side when we scanned the next one. It had 92 printed on the surface. This was a uranium bomb. We inventoried all thirteen storage facilities and registered six plutonium and seven uranium bombs. Now we could plan our core modification processes for these two groups.

We decided that our most challenging device was the plutonium core, and Jane outlined her method by which we would attempt to modify the weapons. "To change this core to the next atomic weight, we have to add a proton and electron to the fifth energy levels. That will change plutonium into americium, which is not suited for a bomb. Doing so successfully will make the plutonium devices inert. We'll have to inject these particles into the core, and neither my team nor I are able to predict the success of this operation. It will be truly a shot in the dark, as you earthlings are fond of saying."

Jane instructed her team to synchronize her systems with the monitor and we were ready to start the trial operation. I directed the focused beam at the center of the bomb, and Jane instructed her team to initiate the proton and electron transmissions. We radiated the bomb for a full minute and terminated the beam and particle transmissions.

"How will we know if we were successful?"

"I have another far-fetched idea, but it's all we have," Jane said. "Let's radiate the core with a low-power energy beam and have my lab analyze the reflection for the radiation level. If we were able to make the change to americium, the radiation level will be substantially lower than the expected plutonium strength."

We waited for an hour. And then we got the enthusiastic message from the lab. "Radiation level low; mission accomplished."

News of the success gave the necessary boost to my confidence that we could complete this mission successfully. The only remaining unknown was now locating the final two devices. I hoped that General Cheong would be able to accomplish that.

The Decision

Now that we were assured we could disable the majority of the stockpile, we informed General Cheong of our status. He decided that we should not draw attention by having him visit our rooms. "Even I am now under surveillance," he told us. "I'm gratified that you can assure me that you can disable the existing stockpile, but we still have to worry about the remaining two bombs that are hidden somewhere. In addition, we have to cripple the manufacturing process. We need to destroy the centrifuges and infect their computer systems with undetectable viruses. We still have a lot of very dangerous tasks ahead of us. We should remain together after dinner and have some security personnel join us. We can communicate with each other via telepathy in the presence of my colleagues, and it will not arouse suspicion. I realize that it will make a conversation more difficult, as we'll be distracted, but we have to be ultra careful," General Cheong said.

That night during dinner, Jane outlined her plan to infect the supercomputers that were dedicated to this weapons development complex. "Our computer viruses are virtually undetectable and are capable of making their own decisions, once they've infested systems," she explained.

"You mean Artificial Intelligence, (AI)?"

"Yes, but they're surreptitious and discrete."

"Sounds like people I know—scheming."

"You can look at it any way you want. After we infect their systems, their development capabilities will be severely curtailed, and they will not recover easily."

"What exactly will the viruses accomplish?"

"They will increase the spin rate of their centrifuges beyond their maximum rpm and destroy them."

While we were planning on our internal intercoms, the rest of the table guests were having animated discussions about the status of the political climate in Pyongyang.

"The leadership is furious about the failure."

"Our 'Dear Leader' was planning to make an important announcement about our scientific capabilities, and it had to be postponed. Our base commander and a number of our top scientist had to appear before the ruling committee and assure the leadership that we would quickly discover the anomaly that caused the misfire."

Good luck with that one. It will be a while before you recover from our visit.

Proceeding

We decided that the most imminent danger had to be eliminated first and made neutralizing the uranium bombs the highest priority. That night, after the dinner discussions, I spent an hour directing our energy beam at the bomb, feeling tremendously satisfied that we were in the process of ridding the world of this horrible capability the North Koreans had.

After the radiation, we used the proven process of analyzing the echo from our special weak signal that was bounced off the core. Little radiation left. Number one was successfully disarmed.

They had seven uranium bombs, and we spent two weeks eliminating this threat to world peace. It still felt strange to me that I was part of this monumental undertaking. I had become conditioned to being a member of our unusual trio, but the implications had never totally sunk in. Now it hit home. I wondered what the outcome of this situation eventually would be for me. I had not forgotten about the bonding discussion that Jane had insisted on having with me. It bothered me on and off that another unknown was looming in my future, and I promised myself that I would force the issue. *When this is over, I'll confront her.*

"I'll be ready," was her answer.

We were able to destroy the bomb stockpile during the following two weeks and could now concentrate on infecting their supercomputer network system, which was on the base. What made this operation easier were the careless connections within the facility that were part of their computing systems. This was a protected, super secure installation with no connections outside the base, and our hosts did not expect hackers to be able to access their systems. The AI computer virus would be gradually introduced. It was a self-propagating set of sophisticated software that would calculate probabilities of success and act accordingly.

I had worked with computers most of my career but had never assumed this would even be possible.

"Welcome to our world," was the dry comment from Jane.

"One thing I don't understand," I told Jane. How do we get access to their systems? We have never been inside their computer facility."

"Their periodic diagnostics are controlled via a laptop that their maintenance technician brings into the computer complex. We've already infected this device. Next time he runs his tests, we're in their system."

Lashing Out

T he People's Congress had unanimously voted to show the world that they were a force to be reckoned with. They announced the next underground test for the following week. It was broadcast with the usual fanfare. The base activities went into high gear, and predictions among the scientist were that this test would be absolutely successful. This time, they would use one of the uranium bombs.

Hate to disappoint you, was my thinking.

The television networks were alerted, and their 'Dear Leader' made one of his appearances, assuring the nation in a speech that this national display of strength would show North Korea's capacity to deter any aggression. The countdown proceeded without a hitch, and when it reached zero, the country held its collective breath. There was only silence. No earth tremor happened, as had been expected.

We were five miles away, having been invited to the VIP viewing stand. Total astonishment and pandemonium was the appropriate definition, after the deafening silence. "This is impossible," was the universal comment.

The viewing stand slowly emptied, and we were driven back to the barracks. I could imagine the fear that was in the hearts of the scientist who would have to explain the reason for this second embarrassing dud. I actually felt sorry for them.

An inspection of all the devices in storage was ordered the next day. Externally, nothing unusual was apparent, and the inspectors were not allowed to dismantle any one of them.

"These are well protected, and nobody can have tampered with them," was the opinion.

The scientists on the base were ordered to undergo polygraph tests, and General Cheong was instructed to double his security detail. They were becoming paranoid.

There were now two bombs left for us to destroy—being held at an unknown storage location. We decided that a cooling off period was warranted and requested that we would be allowed to return to Pyongyang. Our request was refused.

"You may be able to make a contribution when we analyze the reason for this failure. We politely request your assistance," said the base commander.

The refusal wasn't entirely unexpected by me. I just wondered how long it would take before our hosts would become suspicious of us.

· · · · · · · · ● · · · · · · · · ·

Over the next month, they attempted to detonate the remaining bombs we had neutralized—with the identical outcome each time. They were now convinced that tampering had occurred at this location, but nothing could be proven without dismantling the bombs. For some inexplicable reason this was not taking place. Instead, it was ordered that a different test range would be used to explode one of the remaining two devices.

General Cheong conveyed that information to Aaron.

I started to believe that it would be unwise to neutralize the two remaining devices and broached the subject with Aaron.

"If we repeat the process with the last two, they will look totally foolish to the world and will feel that their honor as a nation has been damaged. They will lash out for sure. They have thousands of pieces of artillery poised at South Korea, and I'm convinced they'll start a war. We cannot risk that," I told him.

"This is not a decision for me to make. I'll present our dilemma to the council tonight. Why are you suddenly turning into a dove? I had judged you to be more hawkish," he said.

"Listen, this nation views its military with pride, and they have been thoroughly embarrassed. They will react, for sure."

"Well, this is not up to us," said Aaron.

"I think it's unwise to leave them with any megaton destructive device," was Jane's position. She looked annoyed, but I didn't care.

I have lived here longer than you, and understand these people better than you with your other dimensional philosophies. I was becoming less concerned about her mind reading. *If you don't like it, turn it off. Get used to contrary opinions.* Surprisingly, my thoughts did not provoke a reaction from her.

Aaron did not return that night, and I had a restless sleep, worrying about the consequences of having the North Korean nation lose face with another failure.

Aaron and Jane were waiting for me when I got up, groggy and tired. This situation was beginning to affect me badly. I was prepared for another argument with my hawkish companions, but Aaron cut me short. "The council was divided and, this time, did not vote unanimously. Even though we judged it to be unwise to have them detonate a powerful bomb, we realize that your position is well taken. We're not sensitive about national pride and are always strictly objective. Our goal was to eliminate their arsenal and present them with an ultimatum—demilitarize or be destroyed."

"What do you mean by destroyed? I thought you could not intervene in our earth affairs?"

"When destruction of our world is a possibility, we can change the rules," was his dry comment.

Well, their intervention in earth matters apparently has no limits.

"There's one more condition," Aaron continued. "To get the

council's approval, I had to agree to prevent the North Koreans access to their uranium mines. We're sure their bomb making days will then be over. With the disabling of their centrifuges and closing of their mines, they'll be sufficiently set back."

"Disabling their mining operations may not be possible," I said.

"You'll be surprised what we can do when our own survival may be at stake," Jane said.

"North Korea has rich uranium deposits. The nation currently has seven mines in operation. We'll have to start planning on how to close them without arousing suspicion."

"How do you intend to do that?" I wanted to know. "The mines are well protected by their military; that's for sure."

"We know, but you still don't understand the resources we have to accomplish the task."

"I find that hard to believe, but I'm all ears."

"What's wrong with your ears?" said Jane. "They look normal to me."

I decided not to answer that. It would be like explaining a joke. It wouldn't work.

Aaron had piqued my curiosity, and I wondered what my companions had up their sleeves. "We'll induce earthquakes that will permanently close their mines," he told me.

"That will take a tremendous amount of power."

"We know that and have received special dispensation from the council. You'll direct the power of the strong force directly at the mine entrances, causing catastrophic cave-ins. We know the exact locations and will make sure that each mine will be cleared of workers by creating emergency working conditions. The mine will be evacuated and we'll close it off."

"Sounds impossible to me, but who am I to question you."

"Good. You're starting to finally accept that. When we're assigned a task, we complete it, no matter how difficult."

The Successful Tests

F or this test, one of the two bombs from the second storage location was to be exploded. We weren't sure whether the Koreans were overly cautious or whether they were starting to believe that the twelve bombs had been sabotaged.

It was now a "hands-off" operation for us. We would just be spectators. The security was incredible. They used a modified nitroglycerine truck for transportation. These types of trucks were constructed to transport this highly explosive substance. They have a suspension system that absorbs even the smallest vibrations. Nitroglycerine will explode when subjected to a small shock, but a uranium bomb will not. When I pointed this out to Jane, she attributed the use of the truck to the super paranoid state our hosts were in. "They're not taking chances, no matter how remotely possible another failure is."

Only small a number of the Pyongyang cadre was invited, but a large number of army officials were in the stand with us. It was clear that we were not suspected of having caused the misfires. Only one national TV station was set up on a tower, assuring a perfect view for the audience in the country.

When the countdown reached ten seconds, it was absolutely quiet. Then a vibration became noticeable, followed by a sudden shockwave. The test was successful. The North Koreans were beside themselves with joy. I was sure that some of the scientists realized that they had just received a new lease on life. Some would have been executed as an example, had there been another failure.

We were driven back to the barracks, and the mood of the authorities was festive.

"I think I have to agree with you," transmitted Aaron. "This success will take the pressure off and will allow us to complete this assignment without arousing suspicion."

"I still cannot understand why they don't suspect us. We're the only three variables that are new in this equation."

"I think it is because of General Cheong. The assumption on their part was that he had cleared us for this visit, and their eagerness to obtain our secrets overrode their usual caution."

"We'll still have to be careful with our actions; it's not over till it's over," Jane said.

"Who are you? Yogi Berra?"

"No, I read this expression somewhere, and I liked it. I'm learning all about your language, slang and all," was her remark.

A week went by, and the base returned to normal. We had not seen General Cheong and assumed that we were done with bomb destruction—that was until Aaron received a message from the general. "I have discovered that one extra bomb exists. I don't know the location."

"We should not attempt to destroy this one," was my opinion.

"I don't think we can," said Aaron. "We don't have a clue where it's stored."

I was certainly learning to deal with unknowns.

Using the Strong Force

The Western nations had protested the test, but the North Korean National Assembly issued a statement that it was their right to continue the testing as a deterrent against the unification demands of South Korea and the aggression of Western nations. The United States in particular was singled out as a target for their vitriol.

A week after the test, Aaron decided to investigate the feasibility of triggering a level four earthquake in the vicinity of the largest uranium mine, just to gauge the reaction of seismologists in the country—and worldwide.

"Inducing this kind of shock will confuse them. Quakes like the one we'll trigger usually result from fracking, prevalent in the United States," he said. "The state of Oklahoma in the United States was saturated with these types of tremors when the oil companies injected large amounts of high pressure water into the oil layers."

Natural earthquakes had previously occurred in North Korea, but not close to the uranium mines. That area was not quake prone. The occurrence would be hard to reconcile.

Aaron selected the most important mine and the adjacent milling plant, located in the southern part of the country. The quake would be centered between the plant and the mine entrance. We knew the latitude and longitude of the location and could induce the quakes from the safety of my bedroom.

This time, my companions warned me about the volatility of the strong force.

"We have only limited experience with controlling this immense amount of power. The focusing of the beam requires fifty of our computers to be dedicated to his short duration test. We plan to subject the mine entrance to the full power of the beam for ten seconds and then spread the beam for another twenty seconds. This unfocused beam has sufficient power to start fires at the mine entrance, which will impede efforts to investigate the damage. We will then give them a second tremor, with less power, as the expected aftershock with a normal earthquake. This will convince them it was an unexpected, natural, fault shift-triggered earthquake."

That evening, we assembled in my room, and Jane was in communication with her computer techs.

"They'll closely monitor the output of the beam and have been instructed to terminate the test immediately if fifty of our quantum computers cannot sufficiently control this energy," she told me. "We have never attempted to focus this much power and cannot predict the outcome."

They had made me very tense with their warnings, and I was beginning to think that it was not a smart idea to tinker with the strong force. "Are you telling me that this thing may backfire with unknown consequences?"

"Yes, it's possible that it may trigger a runaway reaction with the uranium-rich deposits. This outcome has been theorized by our scientists."

"How would you stop that, if I may ask?"

"We don't know, but the probability of the occurrence has been calculated as extremely low."

"Well now, that's really great. I'm about to enable a possible catastrophe by setting off a chain reaction, and you still want to proceed?"

"Yes, it is a lot to ask of you, but we must take that chance."

"I'm beginning to believe that you two have been hiding the real reason their arsenal has to be destroyed. Inhibiting their capabilities can't, in and of itself, be enough of a reason to take this remote, but extremely risky chance. I will not agree to operate the display anymore unless you explain why we need to proceed, notwithstanding the possible catastrophic outcome."

My compatriots started conversing on their private link, which did not give me a very positive feeling about them leveling with me. Jane seemed agitated and tried unsuccessfully to hide it, which was another first. She'd never shown emotions before.

"Okay," Aaron said finally. "We'll tell you. We have always refrained from experiments accessing the strong force. Many eons ago, we had a brilliant scientist who insisted that he knew how to harness this energy and requested approval from the council to conduct a feasibility study. He built special hardware required for this demonstration. He would only use ten computers, and he guaranteed the council that the test could be safely controlled and terminated at any time. It was performed in the laboratory of a major technical institution that was located in the center of a large city with three million inhabitants."

I don't think this test had the expected outcome, I concluded.

"It was designed to show our abilities to eventually use this force in order to power our dimension, provided it could be contained. We don't know what went wrong, but the force started multiplying and eventually evaporated the entire city with all its inhabitants, buildings, and waterways. What we conjectured was that, when the computers that were controlling the event were also destroyed, it somehow terminated the process. Nobody survived, and the council decreed that all future research into the possibility of using the strong force was strictly forbidden. Ignoring this would be punishable by death."

"Have you ever been able to duplicate what he discovered and how he accessed this kind of energy?"

"Yes and no. We've developed a theory that points directly at a black hole that was created in this experiment. I'm not sure if you're aware, but those fears were evident when the LHC was constructed in Switzerland. They could not possibly create even a minuscule amount of power required with your existing hardware, but it's theoretically possible. If our rogue scientist birthed a miniature black hole, it may have self-propagated until it exhausted all material that was available. It ran out of fuel and ceases to exist."

"So how were you able to get permission to use the force?" I asked Jane, figuring she controls the computer assignments.

"Because the war machine in North Korea is in the planning stages of starting a nuclear war by dropping one of its bombs on Seoul. That would immediately draw in the United States, and then the other nuclear nations would follow, resulting in a full-blown, global nuclear war, where nations that have them would use their thermonuclear devices. This risk outweighs the uncertainty we have about using a small amount of the strong force to close North Korea's mines. Is that a viable explanation for you?" she asked.

Since Jane had assured me in the past that she could not lie, I had no choice but to believe them.

"What gives you the confidence that we won't create a runaway reaction ourselves?"

"Good question. Our processors have sophisticated software that detect anomalies instantaneously and will terminate the operation upon finding any unexpected occurrence. Secondly, we suspect that the original disastrous effect was caused by using part of the weak force as a catalyst to initiate the reaction. Since then, we have shown with a high probability that the interaction of the weak force with the strong force caused that chain reaction. We will never experiment with this method. Our fifty processors will be able to control this operation. I'm very confident," said Jane.

She walked over to me and put her hand on my shoulder. She looked me straight in the eye with her silvery pupils, and said, "We're a unit, and I'll always be totally truthful with you. I'm part of you and cannot be anything but honest with you. We weren't sure if you were ready to understand the ramifications of our mission, but now I'm confident that you trust us. It's in our own interest to be ultra careful, and we have taken all possible precautions. You must believe us."

I was convinced they had finally revealed their true purpose and decided to agree. "You two have an unusual definition of a partnership, but I'll do my best to accomplish this. Just tell me how to proceed."

Jane's communication link was established, and we were ready.

"Focus the beam at a point away from the entrance."

The image of the mine entrance appeared, with its elevator shaft clearly visible. A number of helmeted workers were also visible. A power indicator was presented on the display, to show the relative beam strength versus the maximum, where we would have to issue the terminate command. I expected the same vibration as I'd felt during my first use of the weak force. But this was different. I felt a mild shock and noticeable heat on my hand.

"Don't remove your hand from the glass," Jane warned. She'd felt my consternation when this unexpected occurrence happened.

"These are the unknowns we have to deal with," was her reassuring message.

The indicator on the display showed 70 percent when we noticed the workers at the surrounding terrain gesturing, and running away from the mine entrance. The tremor had gotten their attention.

"Now, reduce the power to 50 percent and move the beam a few hundred yards. That will start a fire."

I saw flames shooting up where I pointed the beam.

"So far, our results are showing the correctness of the analysis. Let's assume that we can produce the required outcome at full power next week."

"That's sufficient for now," said Aaron. "Let's see what happens next. We just caused a mild quake to get their attention."

I had been apprehensive and was relieved when Jane told me to gradually reduce power. "We need to be sure that we can control the operation by slowly delinking our processors."

On a split screen the monitor now showed the mine entrance again. A few minutes later, the mine elevator got to the top; it was bulging with obviously frightened workers. The next five minutes showed the power output slowly diminishing and finally reaching zero. I was very relieved.

"I'm now confident that we can accomplish this assignment," said Aaron. "We'll give them a few days to put out the fires and investigate the damage."

We observed the frantic efforts of investigators that went on each day and learned from General Cheong that North Korea's seismologists could not explain the unusual phenomena. They had concluded that there must be an unknown fault line deep under the mine.

"Wait until we create the cave-in. That will be a little harder to explain," said Aaron.

Plant Destruction and Mine Cave- In

The fires had been distinguished, and the seismologists were sent home, according to General Cheong. Their investigation had not produced a sensible explanation of the event.

Aaron decided that we would have to concentrate the power of the beam separately on the mine entrance and the plant. "Destroying their capabilities of producing yellow uranium cake is absolutely essential," he said.

"Are we going to blow up a bakery?" I asked as innocently as I could. I wanted to check whether my companions had learned a bit of humor.

When they started explaining that the cake was the product that contained the uranium, I cut them short. "I know exactly what it is," I said. "Don't waste your time."

They looked at me and were obviously confused.

Jane mumbled, "Why ask if you already know?"

I concluded they definitely weren't there yet.

"We're going to concentrate first on the plant entrance and the mine elevator. A mild category four should get them to flee the plant and mine complex. We'll give them an hour to clear both areas. Jane and her people have requested computer capacity for a level six quake, which should be sufficient to destroy each location."

"The plant will be leveled, and a major cave-in will close the mine," Jane added. "It will be over in one hour."

Jane gave me the signal, and I concentrated the beam on the center of the plant's group of buildings. I counted seven major buildings and directed the beam on the largest plant. I again felt the strong vibration and heat in my hand. For a number of seconds there was no visible shaking, but then it started. It looked extremely violent.

"We'll shift to the mine entrance when the buildings are leveled," said Jane. I was surprised at how calm she was. After ten seconds, the buildings collapsed within a few seconds of each other.

"Switch now to the mine and concentrate on the shaft opening," Jane directed. "When we see the cave-in, we'll gradually reduce power, and we'll be done. For good measure, we'll induce a few mild aftershocks tomorrow."

Within a few minutes, the base was in an uproar. They had received word of another disaster in the making. We shut down our operation and went outside to investigate. Our hosts were in an absolute panic. We located the general who was in charge of facilitating our stay at the base and innocently inquired what the tumult was about.

"Another disaster just happened at our primary uranium production plant. It was totally destroyed in another earthquake. We can't understand how this is possible."

We looked at each other and silently agreed. Mission accomplished.

The base did not quiet down for hours, but finally, at midnight, the noise had subsided. I fell asleep, totally exhausted.

The next morning, Jane was waiting for me.

"You okay? You have a tough night behind you.

"It was bit of a strain, I may say."

We repeated the process and closed off the remaining mines. The North Korean seismologists were unable to explain the sudden occurrence of the quakes and resorted to attributing them to unknown faults, deep under underground.

Simultaneous Tests at Two Locations

From what we could gather on the base, their 'Dear Leader' was furious about the destruction of the major uranium resources and he was intent on showing the world that his country was not going to be humiliated anymore. He ordered the remaining two nuclear devices to be detonated simultaneously at the adjacent underground testing ranges. They were spaced twenty-five miles apart. "That's a foolish decision," said Jane. "It shows this regime is up against the stops. If they explode two bombs in close vicinity, it could trigger quakes of unimaginable magnitude. Rational individuals would not play games with those unknowns."

"I agree, but when objections were raised by the general staff, they were threatened with immediate executions; that how it works here. They're all beaten into submission and are just in self-preservation mode," I noted.

"What do you expect to happen when they detonate both devices?"

"Unknown. The test area is not made to survive it. If they're smart, they should minimize the chance of a major quake by detonating the pair in a shallow location, not deep underground."

"A surface test with two bombs will contaminate the test area."

"I don't believe the 'Dear Leader' worries about that. He's far enough away from the location."

As expected, the simultaneous explosions caused the location to be uninhabitable.

$$\cdots\cdots\bullet\bullet\bullet\bullet\bullet\bullet\bullet\bullet\cdots\cdots$$

"It's worse than Chernobyl," I remarked.

"This shows what humankind is capable of," said Jane.

The atmosphere on the base was now difficult to gauge. The commander had orders to evacuate, and we had no idea how we would fit in under those conditions.

General Cheong was no longer certain he could guarantee our safety.

"We won't have a problem disappearing, but you have to get out of here fast. You cannot stay and risk being accused of aiding saboteurs," said Aaron.

Well, this is finally where I'll lose my head. I cannot deny that it hasn't been interesting.

"You're prone to pessimism. You have to lighten up." That was, of course, Jane giving me her five cents worth of advice.

"You aren't exactly the light of the party either, I may say. I'm not clairvoyant, but things do not look promising for the general and me. You two can just depart with the monitor, and we're stuck here."

"We'll find a way. Be assured," was her reply.

Conspiracy Theory

We were convinced that remaining on the base was dangerous. Base leadership had already started to move people to other locations but many nuclear scientists were still assigned to a failure analysis group that been created. If we were again requested to assist in investigating the bomb failures, it would be hard to refuse. Also, the base commander had approached Aaron once for his opinion about the unusual string of earthquakes, but he had quickly made it clear that we had no assistance to offer. A solid scientific explanation would take the pressure off, but Aaron had nothing to offer him. The atmosphere on the base was difficult to judge because everyone was fearful of repercussions. We decided the best approach would be to go on the offensive, and we requested a meeting with the base commander and the senior scientific staff. "We want to share our research in controlling the weak force of the dark matter and assist you in developing the prototype to control it in a lab demonstration. Once you have acquired the ability to manipulate this power, it will be clear to the rest of the world that this country is a force to be reckoned with," we told him. The commander jumped at the prospect of acquiring our research details. "We've become concerned that our results can fall into enemy hands and suggest that the briefings take place at the military academy in Pyongyang. The unexplained occurrences on this base have convinced us that we have to move the meeting to an absolutely secure location,"

Aaron explained. The commander was clearly elated when he said, "I'll notify our general staff of your offer to share your research with us."

"We request that General Cheong be our emissary to brief the general staff and arrange the details. And we have one more important requirement. Accessing the weak force necessitates the utilization of the Chinese collider that's under construction. It is essential that the Chinese be part of the briefings, since their current design is not structured to produce a black hole."

"Nice snow job," I transmitted. "This will arouse some interest and get us off the base."

"I told you we would find a way," Jane said, smiling.

The base commander was beaming when it became clear that our plan would take some pressure off his organization. Accessing the weak force would provide the country with a formidable weapon. It would still be important to determine the cause of the failures, but all eyes would now be on us. "It's a very good plan," the commander said. "I'll make the arrangements for General Cheong and our lead scientist to fly to the capital and brief the staff. I'm sure they'll accept your offer and make the necessary arrangements."

When General Cheong returned from the meeting with the general staff in Pyongyang he briefed the base commander and had a private meeting with us.

"I expected a skeptical reception, but they were immediately in favor of accepting our offer to assist in further developing the collider design and weak force research. There is such a fearful atmosphere since they've have lost their nuclear deterrent that they'll accept any proposal to recover from this devastating condition."

Chinese Participation

That night, Aaron presented his plan to Jane, General Cheong, and me. It had been emphasized again to General Cheong that he would not be left holding the bag, while we escaped.

"Jane and I have planned this out in detail, and you and Wil are going to be appropriately disguised and return to China with their delegation."

"Do I have any say in this? Or am I just a slab of meat in this enterprise?" I said.

Jane and Aaron did not like my comment. "Aren't you pleased that we have found a way to get you out of this predicament?" said Jane.

"That's not the point. If you two have concocted a scenario that will get us out of this bind, I want to hear the details—not the 'don't worry about it; we have it all under control' from the past. Those days are over."

Jane walked over to me and said, "It's not that we're withholding information from you. We're doing this to protect General Cheong and you. Getting both of you out of North Korea will be risky, and we're taking all the necessary precautions. If they suspect anything, they will torture both of you and will use any means to uncover the reason for our visit to their country. Once we have presented the collider details at the academy, we intend to explain our plan to both of you. By now, you should believe that I would sacrifice my own existence to keep you safe."

180

"I think you should believe her," said General Cheong. "No woman has ever told me that."

I knew that Jane and I had bonded during this trip, but I had not expected her to confess to that. I was somewhat shocked and confused. *Is she so attached to me that she would risk her life for me?*

"Yes, I would," was the message from her.

"Now that we're past the drama stage, let's discuss the plan," said Aaron. "Here is what we're going to present to the combined group of Chinese and Korean scientists. We have conveyed that the Chinese are essential, and the presentation will be useless without them. General Cheong obtained information that the scientific collider team from China has been invited to the conference. Things are shaping up."

"Something has been bothering me for a while, ever since we lifted the tank," I interjected. "I'm sure that it made a tremendous impact on the Koreans, and I was surprised that they did not insist on us clarifying how this was possible without any visible equipment. I could not imagine that they would let us get away without providing them the ability to duplicate our demo in their labs."

"Agreed", said Aaron. "In light of their recent nuclear failures, they will not be in the mood to accept our oblique promises. We do, however, have a plan to placate them, and that will hopefully be enough to get you and the general safely out of the country."

"I don't think that leaving us wondering is viable. Since we're the peons in this scenario, we deserve to know how you're planning to play with our lives."

"Have you been reading the classics in your spare time? You're becoming quite dramatic," said the other half of our self-proclaimed unit.

"Well yes, this could be the shortest collaboration of entities from two different worlds in earth history."

"If you two would just lay off the histrionics, I'll explain our plan," said Aaron. "This is what we'll present to them when we explain how we could accomplish the tank demonstration. We've developed a method of capturing small amounts of weak energy and storing the energy in a special enclosure. Think of it as a giant capacitor, like those currently under development for storage of the sun's energy by some of the earth's solar energy laboratories. Our capability has limits, and lifting the sixty-ton tank was pushing the boundaries."

"I guess you can convince them of that fact, but where was the capacitor hidden? Don't you think they were puzzled by that?"

"If they bring this up, I'll tell them that our investors are worried about divulging the construction of this device. It's revolutionary in shape and size."

"More fog balls, yes?"

"Well, it has worked so far," said Aaron. "If you have a better idea, let's have it."

"You can write a novel about your adventure when this is over. That should keep you busy for a while," said Jane.

If I get out of this alive, I may just do that.

Aaron continued to outline his plan. "Elevating the tank was a one-time demonstration, and I'll stress that the energy source was totally depleted. I'll tell them that our funding comes from private investors, and they insist that it's kept proprietary. In due time, the details will be made available. We've filed the patent applications with the World Intellectual Property Organization in Geneva and we don't want the United States and its allies to have access to this information. We've therefore refrained from filing the patents in the United States."

"Do you really think they'll accept those conditions?"

"Well, what can they do? They'll accept them or be without our cooperation."

"I'll tell them that we've been able to interest four entrepreneurs— two from China, one from North Korea, and one from Afghanistan. These investors prefer to remain anonymous for the moment. Their funding allowed us to build a small prototype to demonstrate the feasibility of harnessing the weak part of dark energy. The tank demonstration was intended to prove the feasibility of utilizing this force. The full-size prototype requirements will be discussed in follow-up meetings."

"The success of your plan hinges on their acceptance of your conditions, right?"

"Yes, I intend to outline this at the conference in Pyongyang and will promise to provide as many details as I'm allowed to. The Chinese will be immensely interested in acquiring this information, and I expect them to be cooperative. In a private meeting with the Chinese, I'll explain that the complete scale and details with be presented at their collider facility in China."

"Well, General Cheong's life and mine are now in the hands of imaginary investors. That's comforting." By now I was resigned to the realization that this could be the end of this journey.

"We'll talk later," Jane said. "Let's hear the rest of the plan."

"Producing even a small black hole in their collider will require the majority of the nuclear scientist and engineers from all three partner nations. Our investors have insisted that the three member nations will be allowed to participate in the construction of the collider, or they'll withdraw their funding. We ourselves have to be part of this design and that will assure that Wil gets out of North Korea in one piece. We plan to devise a disguise for the general when he accompanies us. Does that sound like a reasonable plan to both of you?"

"I think it is an excellent approach to blame our restrictions in terms of providing details on private funding. Maybe we should throw in a few bribes along the way," I remarked.

"You're becoming very cynical," was Jane's little stab.

"Why shouldn't I? I'm just entertaining myself. Nobody else seems to have a sense of humor. Why do you think the Chinese won't insist on obtaining the methodology to duplicate what you did at the meeting in Pyongyang?"

"I'll tell them to accept it or forget about the whole deal," Aaron replied. "You can't hold a gun to a mathematician's head and give him five minutes to solve an impossibly difficult problem. This will require close cooperation between us and the Chinese, North Korean, and Afghani scientific teams, as well as enormous financial resources. I'll tell them that, in our estimation, it cannot be accomplished any other way."

"I hope you're right. I'm just wondering how desperate the Koreans have become."

"They will have little choice but to accept our conditions."

"A more immediate risk is getting General Cheong out of North Korea. I would think that he's now becoming an endangered species in his country. A disguise will be necessary to smuggle him across the border into China."

Pyongyang Briefing

The following week, we received the official invitation from the commandant of the North Korean Army academy in Pyongyang: "Your research team will brief our scientists and our Chinese colleagues about your breakthrough discoveries pertaining to dark matter forces."

"We have their attention, and all we now have to do is convince them to accept our recommendation about the teams and location. There will be resistance in accepting the cooperation, but I'm sure that they'll recognize that we hold the winning hand. Without us, they'll get nowhere," Aaron said.

To our relief, General Cheong informed us that he would be in charge of the security team. Apparently, we still had not aroused suspicion.

We requested that we travel by train, instead of the uncomfortable hummer, and the request was quickly approved. A security detail would accompany us, and a special dining car was again ordered for our comfort. We were on our way the next day. It made no stops and arrived at our destination in the afternoon. Comfortable quarters were provided, and I finally started to relax about this dangerous undertaking.

Jane would make the presentation, and she was exceptionally collected. "Not a problem. They're in no position to question me."

We were to present our results in a fair-size auditorium, and it was filled to capacity. I was surprised at the size of the Chinese group of scientist. Theirs was as large as the Korean assembly.

"I think they got the message," I transmitted to Aaron. "It would be a no-go without the Chinese."

"Yes, but there was a strong objection from the Korean ruling council about the participation of the Chinese. Our insistence on the conditions tipped the balance."

After the usual introductory remarks, Jane began her presentation. "We've been instructed by our venture-backed financiers to establish ground rules before we commence with the technical details:

A. The initial investigation must address weak force accessing only.

B. Monthly status reports shall be published in established, scientific publications.

C. Routine inspections by a selected team of observers can occur without prior notice. No military security restrictions shall be enforced during development.

D. Development team members can travel without restrictions. Some audience members seemed to be hyperventilating after she'd listed the stipulations of the financial backers.

"Are you implying that the military cannot be involved in any way?" asked one of the audience members.

"No not at all. As long as the status reports reveal the team members, our backers have no objection to having qualified military personnel contributing to the research effort."

"What will your position be when we have reservations about your ground rules?"

"That's simple. We will present no material of value. You'll have traveled needlessly."

A recess was called to allow the participants to decide how to proceed. They had difficulty reaching a consensus. They conferred with their respective governments during the remainder of the day. There was no mingling. They even had a lunch event that was segregated by country.

The next morning, Jane proceeded with her presentation by first inquiring whether the ground rules were acceptable. A spokesman for both the Koreans and Chinese answered affirmatively.

"Great," she replied. "We have obtained concurrence from our Afghani financial backer and we're ready to proceed. Let's define what's required to develop a prototype. We have discovered that the right combination of uranium and two other available elements in the proper ratios can be used as the target material to produce a black hole. It's not ideal, but better target materials are currently not available. This process is similar to the experimentation that took place to produce superconductors. The composite is the target material in the collider that produces a black hole."

She paused to allow the audience to absorb her requirements.

"When a black hole is created, it's extremely unstable and must be contained with strong magnetic fields. This technology is presently proprietary but will be made available when the patent applications are approved. The current Chinese collider design will be capable of creating a black hole when this composite target material is used."

Jane gave the audience another minute and then continued. "Containing the resulting weak force is challenging. This force can only be controlled with powerful magnetic fields that are shaped appropriately, similar to the cryogenically cooled magnets in a collider. The danger with the containment process is that, if the force cannot be contained, the reaction may become self-perpetuating. To date, we've created a small black hole and have been able to collect the weak part of the force. We've totally refrained from attempting to contain the strong force, which is also produced, in parallel. We strongly urge you not to make any attempts to access this force."

When Jane issued her warning, the audience started loud arguments among themselves. I was surprised that Aaron allowed this and asked him what the purpose was.

"You'll find out in a minute," was his answer.

The obvious leader of the Chinese group raised his hand, and it was clear that his concern had to be addressed. "Before you go any further, we need to know how you produced the weak force energy to lift the Korean tank. You had no collider available, and we have to know how you accomplished that feat."

I had also wondered how she would explain our ability to store sufficient energy to lift the tank. But Jane had obviously anticipated this question. She was her usual cool self when she answered him. "We did have a collider available for the energy collection, and I shall explain the process if you allow me to complete my presentation."

The man sat down, looking upset.

Jane expounded more on the technical details, and it seemed that she had made the desired impression. She provided a taste of the dangers of working with black holes. Mishaps could be disastrous.

· · · · · · · · · · · ● · · · · · · · · · · ·

After two days, the meetings were adjourned to allow the participants time to decide how to proceed. We were informed the next day that we would be allowed to accompany the Chinese contingent to the proposed collider site. They had unanimously decided to designate us as the chief advisers for collider construction and dark energy research. To my surprise, the Koreans had no objections, not even to the stipulation that I would be serving in an advisory capacity. I would be safe. Our remaining worry was General Cheong.

Jane had one more surprise up her sleeve. She still had to answer the member of the Chinese delegation's question about the weak force energy accumulation. When it was evident that the meeting was almost over, Jane addressed the man directly. "General Aiguo, I am now prepared to answer the question you have raised."

I braced myself for what was to follow.

"Do you gentlemen remember the Superconducting Super Collider,

(SSC) that was constructed in the United States in the 1980s in Waxahachie, Texas? This collider was fully functional and was cancelled because of mismanagement and a cost overrun. Prior to the collider's dismantling, we obtained from the US Government a one-week time slot to produce a black hole. We were guaranteed that the ability to contain this powerful force would only be used for peaceful purposes but discovered that the goal was producing powerful weaponry. This misrepresentation caused us to terminate our cooperation. We planned to have enough energy stored for multiple demonstrations but were only able to obtain sufficient energy for the single Korean demonstration."

Noticeable sounds were emanating from the audience. Jane had gotten their attention.

"The SSC was designed to produce forty TeV's but was able to reach sixty TeVs. That was sufficient to create a small black hole. Even with that size, it was sufficient to elevate a sixty-ton tank. That should give you gentlemen a taste of the force's power."

She now addressed the general directly. "I know, sir, that your name stands for 'patriot' and that your intentions are to further the interest of your country. We're prepared to assist you in making this scientific endeavor a great success."

"How do you know my name?" he looked bewildered.

"We came prepared, sir," Jane replied. "It may have occurred to you that I did not discuss the energy storage device. The initial test at the SSC was a feasibility study to ascertain our theoretical design concept. The accelerator produced the weak force, and we've successfully stored it for the past ten years, but we lost about 10 percent due to inefficient storage container construction. We have made giant strides in designing a smaller, more efficient storage device, which we'll use for energy storage when the Chinese collider is operational."

"Have I sufficiently addressed your concerns, General?"

"Yes, thank you very much," General Aiguo said. "I am very impressed by your expertise."

It was clear to me that Jane's presentation had the intended effect. They believed her.

·····•••••◉••••••····

When we were alone, I asked Jane if she had been uncomfortable with her concocted story.

"No," she replied. "I will need this tool, living with you in the future. Twisting the truth is something I have learned from your planet's inhabitants, and I know it can be useful. I've decided to leave my ethics on my planet."

"Was there any truth in what you told them about the SSC?"

"Only that we had three of our scientists working at the SSC from its inception."

"What was their function, monitoring only?"

"No, they actually assisted in the design and implementation of the SSC and were disappointed that the SSC was cancelled. You still seem to believe that we are obstructionists, but that only applies to military and industrial avenues. Pure science we're in favor of."

"Where are your scientists now? Did they go back to your world?"

"No, they're employed at the Fermi Accelerator Laboratory. They are married and have children. They want to stay on earth."

We started to plan a disguise for our friend General Cheong when we got the news. He would lead the security detachment on our trip to China. Eventually, once he had safely left Pyongyang and was across the border, he could make overtures to the South Koreans and indicate he wanted to defect. From that point on, he would be on his own. I was still impressed with the way Jane and Aaron had thought this out.

You people have really infiltrated our world, I thought.

"A politician in the United States addressed a crowd of African Americans as 'you people' and blew his chances to be nominated for president because of this insensitive remark," she said. "Don't treat us with that kind of disregard please."

"What would you like?"

"Don't do it anymore." She was mad.

The distance from Pyongyang to Beijing is 450 miles by train, and we decided again to avoid flying. Some of the Chinese scientists and part of their security detail traveled with us. General Cheong decided to fly with the Koreans and the remainder of the Chinese.

"We don't understand why you opt for the long train ride," were some of the Chinese scientists' comments.

"I wanted to tell them that I valued my life, but before I could utter a word, Jane stopped me. "They consider it an insult if you criticize their infrastructure," she warned me.

Instead, I told them that I was afraid of flying. "As you so nicely explained about adopting our ways," I told Jane, "white lies are allowed under certain circumstances."

We arrived in Beijing after an eight-hour train ride. The dining car had come in handy.

We were met by General Cheong and were escorted to our hotel. The Chinese expected us to remain in Beijing for a long period and had reserved a suite in a plush hotel. We suspected this place was bugged again and we kept our voice communications restricted to praising the way we were treated and conveying our excitement about participating in the collider design meetings. Via telepathy, General Cheong indicated that we were being watched round the clock and should display an enthusiastic attitude toward participating in the state-of-the art endeavor. "Don't overdo it, but be positive at all times. You'll have to arrange a trip to the LHC in Switzerland to brief them on your plans and presumably get the latest details of their design. Since the proposed collider here is advertised to be an international collaboration, they can hardly object to you taking a fact-finding trip. I'm certain that the Chinese will resist having all three of you take the trip, so I suggest that Aaron remains to give them assurance that you'll return, while Jane and Wil visit the LHC. Eventually, when I have safely arrived in South Korea, Aaron can vanish."

Jane's Wish

A aron and the general left my room, and I was alone with my partner in crime. She looked at me for a long time, and I was getting uncomfortable. "Is there something on your mind?"

"Yes, now that we will soon be safely out of here, I want to discuss our future."

"Discuss our future? Isn't that a little presumptuous."

"No, I don't think so. I know you have strong feelings for me, and you'd be unhappy without me. I have thought about this a long time, and as I told you before, I want to be your life partner."

"Do you realize what you're proposing? You're from another world, and from what I remember, you weren't impressed with our bodily contact during the sleeping trial. Being a life partner is referred to on earth as marriage, and it entails more than having our brains linked. It consists of a loving relationship between a man and a woman, on emotional and physical levels. I don't think you understand the importance of that. We couldn't even have children since you cannot conceive."

She was very capable of controlling her emotions, but I saw tears welling up in her eyes. She started to cry, and I felt sorry about my outburst.

"You have to understand that this is rather sudden," I told her. "You have not really displayed much interest in having a connection with me, outside our intellectual one. You've only known me for a short period, and we've been separated most of the time. What you consider to be bonding has serious ramifications. People on earth who are not compatible routinely dissolve their marriages when they discover that they're not meant to be together. That would probably happen to us and would cause tremendous distress for both."

"Well, I realize I have a lot to learn, and I am planning to connect with women from our dimension who have married on earth. We have records, and I'll ask permission to get their names from our archives. I know I'm lacking essential ingredients for our relationship to be successful, but I'm determined to learn and adjust."

"This is not a cooking course, where you experiment with a pinch of this and that. Emotions are not tunable like a radio. They're inborn. I would be very surprised if you find conditions with those couples that turned out to have 'ingredients' as you call them, like passion and physical attraction between the two partners. There is physical love and emotional love, and neither one alone is sufficient for a marriage to survive. It has to be balanced. Book learning in this case does not apply."

"I'm not giving up on us," Jane insisted. And know for sure that I can learn how to make you happy."

With that, she disappeared, and I was alone with my thoughts. All her hinting in the past about having plans for our future and her experiments with the sleeping fiasco should have made me see the light, but alas, I was a little thick myself. Somehow, I had a mixture of a strong attraction and a large set of doubts. I wasn't sure myself how to approach this in a rational way. I remembered when I'd asked Jane at Eddie's house if she wanted to have dinner with us and she'd politely declined. I'd never forgotten her comment: "No thanks. I'll get my nutrition from my own world, and you wouldn't like it if you observed it."

I wondered what else would be lingering in the background.

· · · · · · · ● · · · · · · · · ·

When Jane disappeared, Aaron and I had to deal with the Chinese scientist who busily analyzed the requirements that Jane had left. After two weeks of Jane's absence, I was becoming concerned about her and decided to approach Aaron. I figured he would have some ideas about our unusual situation.

"I have been well aware of the interaction between you and her, and I can tell you right now that I have no advice for you. This is all new for me. I have been inquiring in my world to find a possible solution to your dilemma. Nobody has encountered this situation because you two are the only ones who have connected brains and associated emotions. We're in the dark, just as you are."

Jane appeared after another week, and was upbeat.

"Are you going to tell me what your plans are, or will I have to wonder forever?" I asked.

"I have discovered what is missing in my emotional repertoire and had meetings with our foremost experts in genetics. They suggested that the genes that control emotion, passion, and sex drive are not part of my genetic makeup. I got permission to approach women from our dimension who are living on earth with fulfilling marriages. A few of them told me that they naturally acquired the method to satisfy their husbands and themselves. Others were not able and had to fake it."

I was dumbfounded as I listened to her. "You're really determined to make this work, aren't you?"

"Yes, I'm very much in love with you, and I want you to desire me."

This is beginning to sound like a soap opera, I thought.

Her reaction was fierce. "I'm telling you that I'm in love with you, and you make fun of me. What's wrong with you?" She was standing in front of me, sobbing, and I felt terrible.

"Let me hold you."

Slowly she calmed down. "I found a woman in Germany who has an exceptionally successful marriage. Her name is Gisela Handel, and she agreed to let me take her DNA sample back to our dimension for analysis. Her genome was, as the physiologists expected, identical to mine, except for sixteen genes that were absent in my DNA. Those are the ones that they linked to sexual desire and passion. Gisela gave me permission to have those appended to my DNA helix. I'm now the proud owner of strong sexual desires."

She was standing in front of me and I decided to kiss her, fully expecting the same mechanical reaction from her that I had felt before. I noticed a big difference from her previous way of kissing me. Now her body was involved, and it felt great.

"What happened to you? You never felt like that before."

"That's what I'm trying to explain to you. Gisela's DNA enables me to be the perfect lover for you. Are you happy?" She looked expectantly at me.

"Are you kidding? I'm ecstatic."

I remembered how she'd had no reaction to my touch and had concluded that she had some of the essential connections missing between the usual female erogenous zones in her body and her brain. I casually referred to this as wiring. I was certain that this was beyond her comprehension and decided to refrain from bringing that that up again. That was another mistake on my part.

"I'm aware of that too. It's included in my new makeup."

I decided on a quick test. Kissing her neck produced an immediate tensioning of her body. She wasn't kidding. This was a new sensual part of her that promised to make our interactions mind-blowing for me.

Aaron had discreetly decided to stay away when she dropped this bombshell on me. That she'd implanted someone else's genes in her body in order to give her the ability to have a fulfilling love life was hard to believe. I wasn't surprised that he opted to be on the sidelines. When he showed up, he was all business.

"You and Jane are visiting the Swiss collider next week, and I'll schedule meetings here with the Chinese technical design crew about the initial layout of their collider tunnel design. I expect them to quickly come to the conclusion that its way beyond what they'd expected financially and structurally. Both of you will perform some superficial fact-finding meetings with the LHC crew to convince our Chinese designers that you're collecting valuable data.

The next day, Jane and I bade farewell to our Chinese design crew and we landed in Zurich ten hours later. We were welcomed at the airport by two scientists with zero fanfare.

Reservations had been made at the airport hotel, and we were resting in our individual rooms two hours later. We had adjacent rooms with an interconnecting door. This was not my idea. After a short nap, Jane started poking around in my head.

"Do you want to be alone, or should I join you in your room?"

"I'm tired, but I want to have you near me. Come over and spoon." Before I finished my thought, she was next to me.

"Should we do this during the day?" she said.

"We'll do better tonight. For now, let's snuggle. That will be nice for both of us. I have concerns that I have to get off my chest. I want assurance that the general's escape to South Korea can be arranged. It worries me."

"We're in the process of arranging that," she said with a smile and no details.

"Well, here's my answer to that. So far, we have done well, but I want to make sure that it comes to a successful ending for him. He has risked his life more than I have, and I'm willing to take the chance and become the fall guy."

"You're really becoming very dramatic."

"That may be true, but nevertheless, I want some assurances, and I want to be part of the plan."

"Okay. Aaron is presently arranging General Cheong's escape plan. He'll contact me when it's in place, so relax. Meanwhile, we can discuss our future, after we have successfully concluded this Korea affair."

"Aren't you a little premature in assuming that we're close to finishing up?"

"Soon we'll fill you in on the details. And you can assume that the four of us will be safely in a Western country, having the Chinese and Koreans wondering what happened."

I was getting antsy about this process of smuggling the general and myself out of the country and wondered what tricks these two had up their sleeves this time.

Jane and I were alone during the morning, and fortunately she refrained from disturbing me more with her future plans for the two of us.

"I can wait until you're ready," was her not unexpected reply.

"Please, stay out of my head until I'm ready."

She's so damn tenacious she'll probably ignore that.

"No, I won't," I heard.

After a week at the LHC facility, Jane and I traveled back to Beijing.

Shape-Shifter

Aaron knocked on my door the next morning, and I was ready for an argument. He didn't give me a chance to utter a word. "I know you're anxious to get the general out of this place in one piece, and I'm ready to explain our plan. Just sit and listen."

"Great. You can give the Chinese one of your snow jobs, but how does that affect his escape?"

"From now on, you and Jane will take biweekly trips to Geneva for meetings with the LHC designers. These meetings will be advertised as necessary fact-finding missions. Jane is sufficiently equipped to invent design details that will be believable enough to justify the frequent travel. When the Chinese are comfortable with the situation, we'll make our move."

"And what will the move entail?'

"If you remember from the olden days when we duplicated you, we can copy anything. Keep that in mind when I outline the plan. During your trips, the general always remains here, but he will slowly decrease his interaction with his Korean team and the Chinese. He'll have to invent excuses and remain in his quarters for days at end. He can blame it on the food or being allergic to Chinese women. We don't care. He'll just do it. On occasion, I'll take Jane's place during the trips. You'll always travel with one of us. We cannot rush the process and have to allot at least a month so that they'll get comfortable with this routine. Keep in mind that we're constantly being watched."

"Why did you remind me of the ability to assume another identity?"

"I'm coming to that. When the general's companions are used to his frequent absences because of his digestive spells, we'll make our move. The general will be shape-shifted so that he assumes my exterior features, and you and he (with my physical appearance) will take the last weekly trip. Jane and I will stay behind that day and wait for the signal that you two have safely arrived in Switzerland. We will then quietly disappear and join you. We'll change the general back to his former self, and he can request asylum at the South Korean embassy in Geneva. It will take his team at the collider facility at least a day to discover that he's absent. And if the South Koreans keep his defection under wraps, the North Koreans will only be able to guess what happened." We had taken our trips to Geneva for four weeks before Aaron decided that it was safe to make the final move. I would travel with the general, who would temporarily assume Aaron's physical appearance for the day, while Aaron and Jane would stay behind. Upon arrival in Geneva, we would signal and they would join us.

The Escape

A aron decided to do the shape-shifting in the general's quarters, where he'd assume Aaron's identity. Then he could walk over to my room, where we would depart for the usual weekly trip to Geneva. As the general (disguised as Aaron) stepped into the hallway, one of his security team members was standing outside asking how the general was feeling. Fortunately, General Cheong was able to mimic Aaron's voice and accent and told the man that the general was resting comfortably. He added that no one should disturb him. He was quite ill. The man bought the story and left to spread the news.

Until General Cheong and I arrived at our destination, Aaron had to remain in his quarters, and Jane would interface with the design team.

We had an uneventful flight and arrived in Geneva at eight o'clock that night. I signaled to Jane that we had arrived.

"I knew it all along. I was traveling with you," she signaled.

You should have realized that, dummy.

A short time later, Jane and Aaron knocked on my door. I was happy to see her. Aaron was all smiles and told me to stop worrying.

"Tomorrow we'll hook into the general's quarters at the collider complex and see what conclusions they'll draw about his absence. We'll now restore General Cheong to his old identity, and I'll accompany him to the South Korean embassy. You should bid farewell, because you won't see him anymore."

With that announcement, Aaron and Jane did their hocus-pocus, and the general was his old self.

The process was simple and quick. General Cheong bid us farewell and left with Aaron.

Aaron did not return for hours, and I wondered why he was taking his time.

"It's not a big deal," Jane told me. "The South Koreans are extremely pleased about the General's defection, but they could not understand how we pulled it off. Aaron had to invent a scenario involving Chinese double agents that stretched believability, but they gave up questioning him after a few hours." Their main prize was obviously the general. He was safe, and that had been our objective.

"We don't leave anyone behind—remember," I heard in my head.

Early the next morning, we monitored events at the hotel and noticed increasingly nervous visitors knocking on the General's door. After a few hours, they had the manager open the room, and immediately frantic activity ensued. The alarm was sounded, and his entire security team was ordered to search the premises. Next, they seemed to realize that we had not appeared after the tumult in the hall. They searched our rooms and realized something was seriously amiss. Phone calls were made to the LHC, but we had not appeared that day, and our former hosts were baffled. How could we have left without a trace?

"They'll soon discover that the three of us are safely out of their reach. I can't say that I'm unhappy about having left that place," I added. "All I liked was the food."

I wondered if I was done with the theater I had been involved with. "Can I now go home and return to my old lifestyle?" I said to tease Jane.

"Not yet, but we're getting close to finalizing this affair," said Aaron. The threat to world destruction is reduced by a few degrees but is certainly not eliminated. In the future, some lunatic leader of a country that possesses nuclear weapons may decide to start a first-strike nuclear war. That would invite instant retaliation from other powers, and we'd be right back where we started. No, we have to prove to all the world's nations that it will not be tolerated by us."

Coercion

"How do you plan to accomplish that? Some of these nations don't even have normal diplomatic interchanges anymore," I responded.

"We will contact the US intelligence services and request a meeting with the Joint Chiefs of Staff and the security services. We'll brief them on the methods we used to disable the North Korean arsenal and assure them that we can repeat this with any country's stockpiles. I'll offer them the option to select a Minute Man missile at random, and we'll neutralize the payload. It will be a take-it-or-leave-it, one-time deal. If they refuse, I'll assure them that none of their weapons will be functional in the future," said Aaron

"Can you actually do that?" I asked.

"Yes and no. We could, but it would be costly, risky, and difficult to do. What our warning will produce is enormous uncertainty, and I'm confident that they will want to hear our complete proposal."

"And what would that be, if I may ask?"

"Yes, you may ask, and we'll tell you."

Aaron went to the US embassy and requested that the embassy staff contact Colonel Jack Jones and convey our readiness to meet with his team.

Within an hour we had an affirmative answer. "We'll be in Geneva tomorrow," was the reply.

The next day, Jones and the others showed up. A conference room was quickly arranged, and a guard was posted outside. The cocky Colonel addressed us the instant we'd taken our seats, and I immediately reacquired my dislike of him.

"Have you finally decided that it is in your best interest to cooperate with us?" the colonel said. "If not, we can make conditions difficult for you."

"Well, sort of," Aaron responded. "We're requesting a meeting with your security leaders and Joint Chiefs, where we will define what our definition of cooperating is. We want you to convey that it is of the utmost urgency that we'll be allowed to present our case to your leadership. If you disregard our request, I can guarantee some unpleasant events will take place in the future. These are not idle threats; they are cautionary warnings. You can tell your leaders that dark matter will be discussed at this meeting. That will be all, ladies and gentleman."

The group looked stunned after this short briefing, and Colonel Jones had difficulty keeping his composure.

"You mean we flew here overnight to listen to your empty threats?" he demanded.

"See if you can arrange to be present when we brief your leadership," Aaron replied, "and then you can redefine empty."

With that, he thanked them for responding so quickly to our meeting request, and we left the room, leaving our visitors behind.

"I'm wondering how they will react to your offer."

"Oh, I'm positive that we will have an invite in our hands before the end of the week," Aaron replied.

He was right. The US embassy arranged a military transport for us from Geneva to Washington, DC, for the next day.

"Now the psychological warfare phase begins," was Jane's opinion.

The Washington Briefing

It appeared that the US military and security agencies had heeded our warning not to ignore us, as the room was packed with military and civilian personnel. There were so many stars and gold stripes on the uniforms that it hurt my eyes. The director of National Security gave a short welcoming speech, and we were up. Aaron was the spokesman for our little group. Somehow, I did not feel intimidated by this display of power, which surprised me. I had been battle hardened during my association with Jane and Aaron.

Aaron began with the usual thanks for inviting us, and then he laid it on the line. "As you're well aware, we have visited a number of countries to present our research findings regarding dark matter. Our purpose was not to indoctrinate the scientific communities about our discoveries but, rather, to obtain access to the nuclear stockpile the North Koreans had manufactured."

After this statement, Aaron had to pause, as our audience erupted in loud debate among themselves. They were obviously not prepared for that revelation.

When the noise finally subsided, Aaron continued. "We have used a small amount of dark matter power to totally, and surreptitiously, disabled all their devices. You've been aware of the failures that occurred. We neutralized their weapons."

Aaron had to pause again because of new arguments among the audience members.

"Our capabilities are not restricted to the simple devices the North Koreans had. We can neutralize anyone's hydrogen devices as well. Our purpose was twofold. Eliminate the threat of a deliberate or accidental nuclear catastrophe by the North Koreans and make the other nuclear nations aware of our capabilities. I hereby issue this warning."

He again paused briefly to prepare his listeners for what was to come.

"We urge the United States to arrange a meeting with the current nuclear powers and convey our message to them. Any nation that threatens to use its nuclear arsenal will have its stockpile eliminated. We'll insist on eventual disarmament and will not tolerate refinement of current stockpiles to continue. Do you have any questions?"

The Korean revelation and subsequent warning had the desired effect on the audience. They were having heated discussions, and Jane transmitted to me that things were going well. I was puzzled but decided to wait for her explanation until the meeting was over.

Finally, the National Security director responded to Aaron's warning. "We don't intend to dismiss what you've presented, but we're in no position to give you our response. We'll have to reconvene later this week after we have conferred with our leadership."

"We're available any time for you to provide us with your decision," said Aaron.

Our hosts arranged for a limousine and an hour later, we were comfortably resting in a hotel.

"You should rest for a while, after this stressful day. We'll meet in an hour."

Jane was right. I was exhausted and needed a short nap.

She and Aaron showed up in my room an hour later, and I was anxiously waiting for them to explain how we were going to proceed.

"Can we really sabotage their arsenals?"

"Yes we can, but it's extremely difficult and the outcome would have a high amount of uncertainty. We want to avoid having to resort to that. What we instead are planning is an example of our disabling capabilities. I'm convinced that they will resist any attempt to disarm their weaponry unless we force them with a convincing demonstration. I'll propose to disarm one of their missiles, buried deep somewhere in the US Midwest. We'll invite them to inspect the warhead after our treatment. We'll simultaneously power down one of the nuclear generating stations in the country, momentarily causing a blackout on the East Coast of the United States. Those two events will be sufficient to convince them," said Aaron.

Later that week, we reconvened, and the Director of National Security was adamant. "I have been instructed to inform you that our nation summarily rejects your proposal. Our president's opinion is that you people need psychiatric help."

"I can't say that I didn't expect that reaction, so here is my proposal," said Aaron. "Would you believe us if we provide your leadership with a convincing demonstration? We'll disarm one of your missiles in the Midwest, and your specialist can analyze whether we were successful by dismantling the warhead. That would provide proof of our capabilities."

Again, agitated discussions ensued, and the group called for a recess. I assumed that some urgent phone conversations were taking place.

After an hour we reconvened.

"We agree to let you demonstrate your capabilities. We'll provide you with the location and will shut down the site to avoid harm to personnel."

Within minutes, an air force general handed us the coordinates of the missile silo, and the meeting was over.

We met later that afternoon in my hotel room to plan our next event. I wondered how we could possibly convince this superpower to relinquish its arsenal, and I told Aaron that I would like some answers to reduce my anxiety.

"Okay, we'll tell you right now. Telepathy only please. A hydrogen bomb uses a conventional atomic device as the detonator. We cannot use the same method we used in North Korea to disarm this bomb since we don't know the elements used in the core. In addition, dismantling it will be more difficult since we cannot determine how the atomic detonator is constructed. We'll therefore have to use the strong force to melt the core of the detonator."

"I thought that using the strong force was a last resort," I remarked.

"True, but we can't take chances. We have one shot at this deal, and it has to be successful. It will be challenging, but I think we can accomplish it. When they dismantle the warhead and find it physically destroyed, that should be sufficiently convincing. As an added guarantee, we'll also cause a momentary power failure in the Indian Point nuclear power plant by tripping their breakers at exactly noon. We'll announce the event on the day of the occurrence, to avoid a panic. Those two demonstrations should be sufficient."

Their message was delivered in our hotel the following day. "The consensus of the General Staff is that you should demonstrate your abilities to disable one of our missiles. If you're successful, we'll reconvene the meeting. If not, you can try to sell your snake oil somewhere else."

"Well, that is certainly a well-worded response," Jane commented drily.

"I don't believe they'll be that cynical when we're done implementing our claims," Aaron said.

We had a side meeting with a small group of officials. At this meeting, we informed them of our intention to shut down the electric generating plant. That did not go over well.

"You can't do that," we were told. "It'll cause tremendous problems."

"No more than what a lightning strike would cause," Aaron replied. "We'll cause a power fluctuation for ten seconds, similar to lights flickering during a storm. This will indicate to your leadership what we're capable of and that we don't deal in empty threats. You can inform your leaders that this is meant as a warning."

They left in haste, obviously disturbed by our attitude.

That night, we zeroed in on the missile site from my bedroom. It was abandoned, and warning signs were posted on the perimeter, indicating life-threatening conditions. It appeared that our hosts expected us to detonate the warheads in the missile silo.

"They have no clue what is about to happen to their poor missile," I remarked.

"Just concentrate on the monitor. This is going to be tricky. We'll have to use the power of the strong force to partially melt the detonators without spreading radioactive material over the missile site. These missiles contain multiple warheads, and we must disable all of them."

"What do you mean with *multiple*?"

"These are MIRVs, which stands for multiple independently targetable reentry vehicles. The control circuits eject them at exact points during the trajectory. This will be more difficult than the North Korean warhead destruction. We must carefully control the power of the beam. We can analyze the thermal reflection and stop at 1200 degrees Centigrade. When it reaches that temperature, the internals have been destroyed."

During this process, Jane had been in constant contact with her tech troops, estimating the linking requirements of her computer systems. The thermal reflection indicated the required temperature and we throttled back the power.

"Now we'll sit back and enjoy the spectacle when they open the missile silo."

"How long do you expect them to wait?"

"No more than a few days. There will be no visible damage on the exterior of the missile, and they will have to run their diagnostic computer tests. Those will obviously indicate catastrophic hardware failures, which will then nudge them in the direction of investigating physical damage to their baby. I believe that will be the tipping point in convincing them of our capabilities. Just to make sure, we'll immediately afterward induce the power failure in the electric plant.

After that demonstration, I expect them to invite us for a meeting of the minds."

As expected, the diagnostic test failed 100 percent, and the opening of the missile cone produced astonishment. Most of the electronics had been carbonized, and a visible inspection was sufficient to make believers out of the doubters. We had convinced them that we were serious about our claims.

The East Coast power fluctuation lasted ten seconds and was a mere nuisance—only a flickering of the lights in a number of Eastern US states. It did, however, show US leadership that we meant business.

Now What?

A hasty meeting was arranged by Colonel Jack Jones, and this time two generals joined the discussion. They were of a different frame of mind than the colonel had been. The atmosphere was almost cordial.

Their spokesman, an air force general named Adams, wanted us to explain what our purpose had been for demonstrating the awesome power we seemed to have access to.

"Our purpose is, and has always been, completely nonviolent, with one caveat," Aaron explained. "We cannot allow the unlimited spread of nuclear weaponry to continue and have decided to issue this warning to earth. Any nation that possesses nuclear weaponry is hereby put on notice. Your stockpile will be annihilated without indication to your armed forces that your weapons have been neutralized. If a first strike is attempted with these weapons, they will fail and will immediately invite a devastating counterattack. It should be clear to any rational regime that nuclear wars are invitations to self-destruction if their weaponry cannot be relied on. Our demonstration has been designed to instill this realization."

"We have been asked by our leadership if you're willing to divulge who you are. You seem to have powers that have been unattainable by us, and our investigations have all dead-ended. Who are you people?"

"Please inform your president that I admit to being an alien. That should do the trick."

There was some nervous laughter after Aaron's joke. I don't think our audience was fully convinced that what he'd said wasn't true.

The general continued with his speech. "We were initially disturbed about your intentions but have now concluded that they are peaceful, even though we disagree with your methods. Having induced a power failure in one of our electric-generating plants was particularly disturbing to us."

"We're sorry to have resorted to this," Aaron replied, "but it was necessary to convince your leaders. You can also convey to your president our desire that the United States uses its influence in calling a United Nations meeting," he continued. "This meeting must be attended by all nations possessing nuclear weapons. We're aware which countries possess nuclear armaments, and we'll interpret a refusal to attend the UN meeting as a sign of attempting to circumvent controls. Your president is hopefully convinced that we're determined in our efforts, and the results of our demonstration should have convinced those nations who may have plans to hide their weaponry that doing so would be unwise. We'll take swift action if attempts are made to continue refining existing stockpiles. We're not in the habit of repeating our warnings. Heed this one, or suffer the consequences."

It was obvious that our confrontational approach with them had the desired effect. Everyone among the US contingent was subdued when they left, having thanked us for the explanation of our motives. They seemed to be convinced that we didn't deal in idle threats.

The next morning, we were personally informed by General Adams that the president had sent an urgent message to the UN Security Council president, requesting an immediate emergency meeting with all member nations.

Somehow, the news organizations had received the details of our activities, and the president had to make a speech to the nation to suppress the panic that started to develop.

"Doesn't this bother you?" I asked Aaron.

"Yes, but it can't be helped. We have to make sure that our visit has the necessary impact, and it will be helpful to instill a little fear. Only the threat of obliteration by unknown entities like us will result in positive actions. Even the possibility of mutual destruction in a nuclear war has not stopped the steady expansion of weaponry. Our warnings and the results of our demonstrations are hopefully sufficient to make them realize that they invite disaster if they ignore us."

Jane's Desires

The news leaked out that we were to make an appearance at the UN meeting, and every news organization in the country had front-page articles about the implied threat that Aaron had issued. The coverage was practically nonstop. Pseudo-intellectuals were spewing their knowledge over the airwaves, and religious fanatics were forecasting the end of the world. We had invitations for interviews galore, but all were politely refused.

"Wait for the UN presentation. We'll make everything clear."

We were informed that it would take a week for all member-nation representatives to arrive in New York City, and I was getting bored. It appeared that I was now conditioned for daily excitement. I just looked at some interesting movies on TV and read a bit. I was beginning to wonder when Jane would drop another zinger on me. It had been weeks since her last bonding discussion, and I was convinced that she had been serious about her desire to spend her existence with me on earth. *Could she have had second thoughts or been prohibited by her superiors from pursuing our connection?*

To my surprise, I found myself longing for her presence, even though I simultaneously was stressed out about the insane existence she had forced me into. Until the North Korean affair, I had been reasonably conditioned and had adjusted well, but events during the last few weeks had severely disturbed me. The three of us taking on this superpower, with our threats and making speeches to the United Nations, had exceeded my wildest imagination. I was certain that US intelligence agencies would be conducting background checks on me, and I wondered if they would uncover Eddie's residence. Now it made sense why they had requested him to not be privy to my brain fusing procedure. Questioning Eddie would lead nowhere, since he knew nothing. As I was relaxing, my partner decided to return. "I sensed that you missed me, so here I am."

"Well, do you have a follow-up for your somewhat unconventional proposal for me?"

"Yes. That was the reason for my long absence. I had to overcome strong opposition to my request to bond with you. That, however, was the easy part. Many of our world's inhabitants have been what you call married, but they were not as critically important to my world as I am. If we're married, I have to resign as a member of the council, and a replacement has to be found. I have been in charge of the science division in my dimension forever, and my leaving is disturbing to the council. However, that was not the major obstacle I had to overcome. Are you now prepared to listen to the addendum to my bonding proposal?"

Why not? By now, I don't think you can floor me anymore, no matter what your desires are.

"Well, I want to make a child with you." She actually planted this directly in my brain. No chance to misinterpret that.

I had been wrong, as usual. She had managed to floor me again. "Have you gone off your rocker? We just had one night of sex, and a minor detail is that you can't bear children. And what do you mean by *making*. Do you manufacture kids in your world?"

"Let me explain," she said calmly. "You're incredibly excitable."

"Well, at least one of us is."

"We have about reached the end of our journey together. Aaron is returning to my world, and I'm staying with you. I want us to continue as team of three, rather than two. Our son would be an ideal candidate, since we can mold him after the best of our genetic makeup. You interpreted my desire for having a child as having a baby, but you're overlooking one fact. Our child can be of any age, and he can have all of your genetic characteristics or all of mine or a combination of both. We can decide on his genetic makeup and also what age he will be when he's born. This is the normal procedure in my world, and it simply requires following an established set of formalities. He can be here next week, if you grant me this fervent wish."

"Would this mean another extraction of my DNA?"

"No physical extraction; our genetic pools are in place. All it requires is your approval. And there is one more thing. Our scientists were able to synthesize the genetic sequence that I obtained from Gisela Handel in Germany. They analyzed it and found some puzzling and unexpected deviations from the norm. This woman's set of genes that corresponds to passion was difficult to decipher. It contained both physical and emotional aspects. Gisela indicated that she was very much at ease with what you refer to as lovemaking and had no difficulty satisfying her husband. That's why I now can love you to my utmost abilities."

I was stunned by her matter-of-fact details about producing a son and happy to learn that her DNA changes would be refined even more.

"What age would our prepackaged son be when he arrives here?"

"Well, you just turned thirty-six years old, and I assume you were virile at the age of eighteen. He can be eighteen years old too."

"Same age as the maker would be," I remarked drily.

She was more emotional than I had ever seen her before, and I had trouble wrapping my mind around the events that were unfolding before me. The conflicting pros and cons that I suddenly had to deal with were testing my usual, relatively objective mind-set. Getting married to an alien and becoming a father during my reborn existence? My realistic nature was being sorely tested. I knew I could hold Jane off for a while, but she would be persistent and convincing. I had developed a physical and emotional attraction to Jane, and I was sure I wouldn't be happy living without her. Craziness aside, she had great qualities. I didn't want to make an impulsive decision and told her that I needed time to digest the future outlook for us.

"Fine, but don't take forever. It is hard for me to live with the uncertainty."

She had really shaken me up with the outpouring of her emotions, and I had not expected that. Could I live with her and a son who would never age while I slowly deteriorated? It was a confusing and disturbing prospect for me. I definitely needed time to evaluate this jarring offer she had made.

Aaron's Explanation

A UN courier delivered the message addressed to Aaron.

"We hereby assert that your presentation to our member nations is scheduled for the morning of March 20." That happened to be my old birthday. I wondered what kind of a birthday present that was going to be.

We had two days to prepare, and I decided to take advantage of the lull before the storm, resting in my room and contemplating the outlandish proposals Jane had hit me with. She had decided to return to her world, and Aaron was in his room, relaxed as ever.

"Do you ever worry about anything?" I asked him when he came over to check on me. "I'm very nervous about this business, and you seem unaffected, even though you'll soon be addressing a global organization. Does anything ever disturb you?"

"The only time I was on edge was when we met in Holland, at the flea market. Everything depended on you, and I was worried about the outcome. We had confidence in you but also realized that there was an uncertainty factor that could have derailed our plans. That made me nervous."

Well, that almost sounded like a confession. I never expected to hear him admit that they hadn't been 100 percent convinced that I would agree to cooperate.

"You would be surprised to learn that we're not that different from you in our emotional makeup. In our world, we're trained from early on to suppress illogical behavior, if it can adversely affect the outcome of events. We analyze and decide, based on probabilities."

"Are you an exception, or are all your inhabitants of that frame of mind?"

"All are, but we're also individually capable of overriding those decisions if the outcome would be beneficial. I know why you're questioning me along these lines. You're worried about your future with Jane, should you decide on accepting her plans. I'm no expert in these matters, but I can tell you this. Jane has sacrificed her status and position in our world to be your partner, and that was totally unexpected by me. She achieved the highest status, which was previously only attained by men, and she's offering to forego all that to be your life's companion. Initially, I was convinced that this was momentary, irrational behavior, but I have changed my mind. She once told you that she'd sacrifice herself for you, and I know you were skeptical. I sincerely hope that you're now convinced. She has made the decision, and it cannot be undone."

Hearing from Aaron what Jane was abandoning in her world to be with me made me realize the momentous sacrifice she had made in deciding to start a new life with me. At that moment, I decided to accept her proposal, baggage and kid included.

The United Nations

J ane arrived the morning of Aaron's delivery to the nations of earth. We were driven in a motorcade from our hotel to the UN Secretariat building, and the roads along the route were all barricaded by New York City police and military personnel. I was convinced that most New Yorkers disliked us by now because of the traffic jams created by our visit.

Upon our arrival, I was taken aback by the representation of nearly every member of the UN organization. It wasn't just the major nations with large, standing armies. Even the small countries that still defended themselves with bows and arrows were present. *Amazing*, I thought. *We really have gotten their attention with our threats.*

When we entered the building, we were intercepted by two US generals, who made a last-minute attempt to convince us not to reveal the full extent of our intentions. "Threatening the nuclear powers of the world with your capabilities will have a detrimental effect on the status quo we've arrived at. The threat of mutual destruction has been successful to this point. Why fix something that isn't broken?"

Aaron's opinion was different and he told the generals that he would present our case in detail. "If that is not sufficient, you're beyond help."

I was sure it had been a long time since these generals had been spoken to like that. They were clearly intimidated.

After the expected welcoming speech, it was Aaron's turn. He had told me that it would be difficult to convince the gathering of our capabilities without giving them assurance that we would indeed neutralize their arsenals. "I'll hit them hard up front," he'd told me.

············●···········

"Before I start outlining our demands," he began, "I want to make it clear that we're not members of any organized Gandhi-esque passivist organization. Without clarifying who we are, I want to make it abundantly clear that we're determined to put a halt to the insane arms race a number of your nations are pursuing. If this warning is not heeded, we will take more convincing actions that will have detrimental consequences. Do not assume that we're not capable of implementing our threats. It will be decidedly unfortunate if you plan to test our determination."

Translators had difficulty overcoming the loud arguments emanating from the audience.

"I'll now provide some evidence about the conditions we have caused in North Korea in the past weeks. Their nuclear arsenal was destroyed by us, and we caused the devastating earthquakes that closed the North Korean uranium mines and processing plants. Our intentions were twofold—eliminating the threat to world peace and destroying their supply line to terrorists. As you saw by the repeated failures of the devices, we were successful in thwarting the detonation of their weaponry."

The noise from the audience was so loud that the secretary general had to threaten to delay the meeting. That did it.

"The North Korean scientists were unable to determine the cause of the malfunctions. That's because we're capable of similar destruction of any arsenal without your knowledge. The incapacity of your weapons would only manifest itself if you were unwise enough to start a war." Aaron gave the audience a few minutes.

"You may also be aware of the momentary power interruption we have caused in a US nuclear power plant. In addition, we have provided the US Armed Forces a demonstration of our intentions when we detect our warnings are ignored. We will not provide details, but it suffices to know that today's gathering is the result of our recent demonstrations. As of today, all nations are hereby notified. Any nuclear power, now or in the future, will have its arsenal neutralized without warning. The neutralization will not be evident, but choosing not to heed this warning will have devastating consequences—ones that will become immediately clear when any nation attempts to use its disabled weapons, whether provoked or not. We urge all members of this organization to dismantle their stockpiles."

This definitely got the audience's intention. Aaron had purposely made his speech brief, and he left everyone wondering who we were and whether we could actually follow up on our warning.

The US generals attempted to corner us again, but Jane waved them off. "You've heard what we intended to convey, and we're done talking," she told them. "You know our position, and further discussions are useless. Our warning is irrevocable."

Wow, that was pretty brutal. I had not thought that she'd be that direct, I thought.

"How else did you think I could have got attention?" said Aaron. "Nothing other than a direct threat to their existence can convince them."

"Do you think that we got the message across to the nation's representatives?"

"If they still have doubts, I'll offer one more demonstration of our powers. I'll give them the choice between grounding their aircraft, shutting down the nuclear propulsions of a large part of their submarines, or inducing a powerful quake in the area of their choice. This promise should give their presidents a few sleepless nights, and will be convincing enough for them to initiate future disarmament conferences."

Incarcerated

T he day after the completion of the UN meeting, I was cornered by Jane in my hotel room.

"Have you made a decision about our future yet?"

"Yes, I have. I was actually sober when I convinced myself. We will be a unit, a team, a triple—however you want to define our connection. I have no idea what I'm getting into with you, but I think I'll be up to the challenge."

"Well, that is about the most unromantic response I could have imagined," she said, but she was obviously elated.

I was glad I had overcome my indecision. I was sure it would take a while to get over my doubt that this experiment would be successful. Jane loved assigning her probabilities, and my factor for success was barely at the 50 percent level. I wasn't planning to divulge that to her, but I screwed it up anyway.

"Mine is 100 percent," she said.

"Now that we have decided, when will I see our offspring?"

"I hope to introduce him to you within a week. I'll have to do some arm twisting to get this approved, but you'll meet him soon."

Aaron and Jane had left, and I was left alone in my room with my thoughts.

· · · · · · · · · ● · · · · · · · · · · ·

To my surprise, I had no visitors from any official US agency during a full week. I wondered whether the US government had decided to accept Aaron's ultimatum. As a minimum, I expected some requests for clarification and a definition of timetables.

None of that occurred until a day before I assumed Jane would return with my offspring. This time, six FBI agents politely knocked on my door and forced themselves in when I opened it.

"Looking for something?"

"Yes, we have to inform you that you are requested to accompany us."

"Do you have specific charges against me?"

"We'll read you your rights, and then you can obtain your lawyer."

We were on our way out of the building when Jane contacted me via telepathy. "I'll reach Aaron and we'll take care of this situation quickly," she assured me. "Don't worry; they can't prove anything against you."

I was loaded into a black van and driven to an impressive-looking building. To my surprise, Colonel Jack Jones was waiting for me with a number of sinister-looking individuals. I smiled at him, and he shook my hand. "This wasn't my idea," he said. "It is out of my hands."

"Well, if this is the way your authorities think they can get information from my colleagues, I wish them luck. It'll be counterproductive. That I can promise. This may turn out to be a short incarceration that will produce only antagonism from my companions. I urge you to inform your superiors that they should reconsider their course of action."

They left me alone in my room, with an armed guard standing outside the room. A little later, Aaron and Jane appeared in my room. By now, nothing startled me anymore, and I acted like I expected this.

"Don't be so cool. I know we shook you up a little with our sudden appearance," Jane said with a twinkle in her eye.

"Okay, all conversations nonverbal," Aaron interjected. "I intend to visit the president tonight, when he's alone in his residence, and convince him to cooperate with us rather than resort to strong-arm tactics. My appearance in his well-protected quarters will be sufficient to convince him that our demands should be taken seriously. I'll issue a vague warning about consequences, and that should be enough. If he doesn't realize that we're not to be toyed with, then nothing will convince him. My appearance at will in his room ought to be enough for him to realize that we have extraordinary powers. Tomorrow, I expect them to release you. I'm leaving now, but Jane has elected to spend the night with you. I'm aware of your imminent joining ceremony and fully understand that this is normal on earth. Personally, I do think you two are nuts, as they say on earth." He laughed and was gone.

I was alone with my future spouse, and the situation was awkward.

"Are we sharing the bed in this room, or do you want me to disappear?"

"Well, let's see what your new hormone set can do for us."

The lovemaking was mind-blowing. She not only responded to my initiation but actually controlled most of it. Not in my wildest dreams could I have imagined this. She thoroughly wore me out, to the point where I had to ask her to give me a break.

"I thought you had more stamina," she teased.

We spooned and I fell asleep.

The next morning when I woke, she was looking at me and asked if I was satisfied with the DNA transplant.

"Satisfied isn't the right word, sweetheart. I'm thrilled out of my mind. We should send a thank you note to Gisela in Germany."

"I enjoyed the new intense feelings very much but was confused that I seemed to lose control of my responses. They became involuntary. Why do you think that happened?" she said.

"It means that your human genome addition is doing its job. It is called passion, honey."

We heard noises in the hallway, and she quickly kissed me. In a second, she was gone.

It was Colonel Jones again, along with the two generals, who walked into the room. They seemed now to be the intermediaries between the US government and us.

"We have been instructed by our superiors to inform you that a dreadful mistake has been made. A misunderstanding between agencies has been the cause. Our president personally assures you that you're welcome to remain in our country, without any interference."

The message was short, and to the point. Whatever Aaron had discussed with the president had produced the expected results. The United States had decided to play ball with us.

Jones and the generals offered me a limousine, but I declined. Jane had informed me telepathically that she'd be waiting outside the building.

"Now that I have been released, let's go back to the hotel where we can discuss our future in more details," I suggested.

We left the government building where they'd held me and were soon in the comfort of my hotel room.

The Introduction

"Would you like to meet your son now? I can summon him right into your room."

"You mean he has the same abilities as you and will not be restricted to living as a mortal individual with me on earth?"

"No, he's virtually a copy of me, with my intellectual powers, along with parts of your DNA, including your moral and emotional makeup. He's truly our son."

"Well, it's now or never," I said. "Uncertainty has never been my choice in situations. Let's have the introduction."

Our son appeared within minutes. He was a strapping, six-foot tall, great-looking individual, looking somewhat confused as he appeared before me. He looked expectantly at his mother, but she made no motions toward guiding him in his next move. The situation was rapidly becoming awkward, and I started to feel sorry for the poor kid.

"Hi. I'm you father," I said to break the ice. "We'll be together for a while."

I then asked Jane if he had a name yet.

"No, I wanted to discuss that with you."

I had given that detail no thought and told her that I would leave it up to her.

"I like the name Xenon. It is an old Greek name and stands for 'receiver of life from Zeus.'"

"Wow, is Zeus your machine he was made in?"

I instantly regretted my stupid thoughtless response, but it was too late. They both reacted by disappearing from the room.—Returned to their own world, no doubt.

· · · · · · · ● · · · · · · · · · ·

For a week, I floundered in my room, worrying about whether I had permanently destroyed my relationship with Jane and our son. I had no way of contacting her, since communicating telepathically between our worlds required the advanced capability that I didn't have. Finally, in my agony, I decided to try communicating with her via the monitor that was left in my room. It had been my constant companion ever since I'd become its owner. Aaron had always stated that it should be close at hand for me, just in case we needed it.

When I touched the screen, I got an instant response from Jane's technicians.

"Is anything wrong? We have been informed that this connection would not be used anymore."

"Yes, something is seriously wrong on my end, and I need to urgently talk to Andryna. Can you please get her on this connection? It's very important." After an impossibly long wait, the tech returned and said she was not available.

"Is there any chance you can find Anryna?" I almost asked for Aaron and realized at the last moment the technicians knew nothing of the nicknames we used here on earth.

"He's not available either."

"Okay, then tell him to pick up the monitor at his convenience," I said. "I'm going back to my old residence to relax with my older self. It has been nice working with you guys."

I shut down the connection and went to bed. I was barely asleep when Jane shook my arm. "You cannot back out of our agreement."

She was furious, standing in front of me, her eyes seemingly boring into my soul.

I was instantly awake, and made a futile attempt to defend myself. "I tried to apologize, but you disappeared before I could say a word."

"Well, what you expressed is identical to comparing our son to an animal. How would you like that?"

"Why don't you connect with me and gauge my feelings right now. I feel terrible about what happened. It won't ever happen again."

She looked at me for a long time and slowly started to calm down. Aaron and Xenon had been in the background watching the spectacle, and it was clear to me that they had no clue what to make of the interaction between Jane and me.

Aaron finally broke the silence. "If you two are going to be all right together, Xenon and I will depart. This was enough drama for both of us."

"Tomorrow we'll have a long talk, I promise," I said to my son as they disappeared. I wasn't sure he'd heard me.

"Come sit with me," I told Jane. "I want to hold you. I felt miserable without you and feared I had destroyed our bond forever. Can you please forgive me?"

"Well, when I felt your emotions, I knew that you honestly felt sorry, and I forgave you then. I just thought you should worry a little longer."

She had a refined way of torturing me. I wondered if those characteristics had also been transferred from the earth gene donor.

The next morning Aaron and Xenon appeared, ready to discuss our next move.

"I'm returning to my own world, and I'll leave you three here to have a peaceful existence for a while," Aaron said. "It has been a challenge for me to adapt to your environment, but the positive outcome made it worthwhile. I have important tasks in my dimension that require urgent actions, and I'm not needed here anymore. Before I go, I have one piece of information. The council approved Wil's ability to use the advanced telepathy level, with one minor restriction. Jane will have a barrier installed that will prevent Wil from sensing anything other than Jane's emotions. In the future, this will enhance Wil's communications between you, Jane and Xenon. I hope that's sufficient for both of you," he said.

With that, he shook my hand and was gone.

I was alone with the rest of my family. I was getting uncomfortable with the situation, realizing that carelessness with language had to be kept at bay. I did not want a repeat performance of my earlier faux pas.

"Do you have any plans you think we should discuss?"

"Yes," Jane replied. "You'll have to spend time with our son, to give both of you a chance to get to know each other. I'm still learning how to live with you, and it is essential that we avoid misunderstandings in the future. I want to go to Las Vegas and get married, the earth way."

I had seen this coming and was not totally shocked. "What does this do to your status in your world?"

"I'm important enough to coerce them into accepting my behavior."

Wow, she must be a big wheel.

"Yes," she replied. "I'm not just the wheel; I'm the whole vehicle. Will you accept me as your spouse?"

I did not have to ask anyone for her hand in marriage and quickly agreed.

"Absolutely and of course," I said.

"Great. It will be a simple civil ceremony, with our son giving me away. That will add to our family bond."

It was clear that she had planned this for a while, and I couldn't say that I had any objections. We would be a troika.

Settling In

O ne thing had puzzled me for a while. How did Jane and Xenon plan to finance the living expenses we would have. I had some independent income and a small amount of savings, but it was insufficient to support all three of us. My funds would also have to be shared with my old self, who was living a peaceful existence in my old residence.

"How are we going to afford living together?" I asked Jane. "I can't even pay for the airline tickets to Las Vegas."

"Not a problem. I have a large number of diamonds with me that we'll cash in tomorrow. Xenon and I will take care of that in Antwerp, Belgium. We'll have sufficient financial resources for our future."

"How were you able to accumulate all that wealth?"

"In our world, diamonds are a worthless commodity and not particularly useful for anything. They're abundantly available and have no value. I can bring unlimited amounts here, and we'll be able to live comfortably in our new lifestyle."

"In that case, we should discuss where we want to settle in the United States. I would like to stay close to my other self, since he's advancing in age."

"Yes. Xenon and I have already agreed that whatever you choose will be fine with us. We can adapt to anything."

They left early in the morning the next day and returned in the afternoon.

"The diamond expert in Brussels nearly fainted when I gave him a handful of stones to examine," Jane told me.

The trader had told her that the diamonds were of the highest quality he'd ever seen in his entire career. He'd been in the business for forty-five years, and her collection's quality was a first.

"I told him that we would keep him in mind for future transactions. The man was ecstatic with the large commission he made. Afterward, we visited an international bank and deposited the check we received at the diamond exchange. We're now official millionaires."

My capacity for being surprised had been blunted by my exposure to Jane and Aaron and their dimension, but this flipped me out. Becoming instantly wealthy was beyond my imagination. Jane showed me the deposit slip, and there it was. We had a checking account in both our names with a one and seven zeros.

The next day we flew to New York and checked on Eddie. It was as if we had left yesterday.

"Anything happen while we were gone?"

"Not really," Eddie said. "How are things with you folks?"

"Same old spiel with us. Nothing out of the ordinary happened," I told him.

"Good decision to tell him as little as possible. You never know what will happen in the future," Jane said.

"Do you have anything in mind that'll keep me awake at night?"

"Not yet, but I'll think of something."

A week later we took a quick trip to Las Vegas and arrived back home a day later as a married couple.

Xenon was integrating rapidly and had made a number of friends. He decided to enroll at a university in Connecticut and told us the coursework was not challenging but enjoyable. He told me that he liked the camaraderie at the school and had met an interesting female.

"It's nothing serious like you and Mom, just friendship."

Good luck with that. I know how it goes.

Jane and I continued discovering each other, and we were content. Mealtimes were always an adventure. She slowly started to taste some of the food I had prepared for myself, and after a number of bouts with indigestion, she found the right combination. We could have meals together and also enjoy a glass of wine. She sipped, and I did not.

She hinted that with our capabilities and the monitor that was my interface to her world, we could put our abilities to good use.

"Do you have anything particular in mind?"

"Don't know what yet, but I'll think of something."

"That sounds great. Let's have a glass of wine and sleep on it." I was in no hurry to get on the road again.

We purchased a comfortable house close to Eddie's residence and settled into a restful, not very exciting existence.

I resorted to adapting to my old lifestyle again—Taking it easy, hanging with my old self, and looking at TV.

This quickly became a drag for Jane and me, and I suggested that we should travel the world. Maybe we would get some ideas about what to do with our spare time.

On our journeys, we encountered many inequities and a great deal of misery, and we slowly realized that we could force corrective measures.

"Do you think we should take action in the future?" she asked.

"Why shouldn't we?" I replied. "I live only once."

"I wouldn't count on that," said Jane, giving me her seductive smile.